OPERATOR 5:
SCOURGE OF THE INVISIBLE DEATH

SECRET SERVICE OPERATOR #5™

AMERICA'S UNDERCOVER ACE

SCOURGE OF THE INVISIBLE DEATH

By Curtis Steele

STEEGER BOOKS • 2020

CHAPTER 1
ARMADA OF DEATH

MILLIONS THRONGED the streets of New York and the coastal cities of New England to see the greatest display of armed air power ever held in the United States.

They gazed into the clear, blue sky impatiently awaiting the appearance of the gigantic, aerial parade. For long weeks the newspapers had heralded the tremendous demonstration of the nation's battle birds planned for this afternoon. Countless eyes lifted from every park and available roof and window as the moment approached when the winged armada would come roaring across the zenith.

The mighty review was calculated to reassure a people haunted by a growing fear of impending catastrophe. While the flames of war raged in Ethiopia, the airplanes of the army and navy were to thunder a promise that the United States would not become involved. While all Europe smoldered, ready for bloody conflict at any moment, the American aerial armada would display our strength to the world. Today the multitudes who dreaded a new World War would see how swiftly the wings of our new sky defenses could spread protection in the event of a national emergency.

The careful plans of General Staff would send the powerful air corps crates swarming off every field along our northeastern coast. Painstakingly coördinated instructions were to form

hundreds of bombers, pursuit ships and combat planes into a winged cavalcade which would howl its way along the seaboard in a series of dazzling maneuvers. For weeks, the moment had

Without the slightest warning, doom
struck the great armada of the air!

been awaited when the President's signal would launch the inspiring review into the sky. Now the moment was at hand....

Radios, operating in countless homes and automobiles, broadcast the voice of an announcer speaking from Washington, D.C.

"The President is at his desk in the White House, ladies and gentlemen. Before him is a golden telegraph-key. Wires lead from it to the fifty-seven army forts and the twelve air-fields where our planes are now waiting. All commanding officers are ready. The President's touch on the key will send hundreds upon hundreds of battle planes into the sky. He is about to speak. The next voice you hear will be that of the Chief Executive of the United States!"

"My friends," the kindly, confident tones followed at once, "we have labored long and diligently to build up the defensive power of our nation. We were weak, but now we are strong. Let us rest assured that our homes and our families and our jobs are safe from the ravaging of any aggressor. Today, the whole world will witness that we are a diligent guardian of the destiny of our people. It is with unbounded pride that I now order our great air fleet to pass in review before you!"

The announcer explained breathlessly: "The President is flashing the signal! The mighty demonstration is beginning!"

THE MULTITUDES in New York, and in the cities along the New England coast, watched the pale sky with new eagerness. During the long minutes which followed, no plane came into sight except a few commercial craft chartered by the major broadcasting chains. The announcers in the pits, circling over the air fields, watched developments during the unexpected delay. Their voices reflected the growing disappointment of the waiting millions.

"The President's signal has been received, ladies and gentle-men, but apparently some confusion has developed. We under-stood that the United States planes would begin flight at once, but none of them has yet left the field directly below us. We can see the pilots in their pits, but for some reason the take-off order has not been given. We will continue to circle until this unit launches into the air."

Repeated announcements increased the misgivings of the restless crowds. News came from field after field that the great parade of the air had not yet started. After many anxious minutes, the sky was still empty except for the incessant circling of the broadcasting ships. The flying announcers fumbled with words in their attempts to cover the delay. Their hesitant excuses only emphasized the shocking fact that the widely heralded maneuvers—a display intended to demonstrate the swift action possible for our new air forces—had faltered at the very outset!

On Miller Field, Staten Island, New York, a stern command-ing officer stood beside his ship, watch in hand, peering baffled into an empty sky. Major Anthony Masson, in charge of the squadrons assigned to this base, had received detailed instruc-tions outlining his part in the winged cavalcade. His take-off had been scheduled to the second to synchronize with the flight of units from other airfields. Now he found his orders completely disrupted. The zero moment had passed.

Smart lines of planes were waiting on the field, their bright propellers flashing. Pilots were sitting uneasily in the pits. They were ready to go into action the instant their commander's signal was given—but it did not come. Every aviator's gaze was directed at Major Masson during that unnerving wait—including that of a young man in flying togs who stood quietly near the operations-office.

Half an hour before, he had circled over the field in a flashing pursuit ship. He had landed at the edge of the tarmac and presented a communication to Major Masson which was signed by Major-General Falk, Chief of Staff. It stated that the bearer was granted special permission to fly with Masson's unit in the air parade—without actually becoming a part of it—but it offered no explanation of his mission. It stated further that the communication facilities of the field were to be placed at his disposal if he so requested. Mystified at the extraordinary orders, Major Masson had fired impatient questions at the young man, who answered by displaying a credential—enclosed in a thin, silver case—which had immediately satisfied the major:

THE WHITE HOUSE
Washington

To Whom It May Concern:

The identity of the bearer of this letter must be kept strictly confidential.

He is Operator 5 of the United States Intelligence Service.

The signature affixed to the letter was that of the President of the United States.

THE EXISTENCE of the undercover agent designated

Operator 5 was known to many high-ranking officers of the army and navy, but few of them had ever met him face to face. Though he had investigated and solved many dangerous cases of the utmost importance to the United States Government, his work demanded the closest secrecy. His exploits were the subject of exciting rumors among federal officials, for it was recognized that he was the ace investigator of a service which functioned almost unknown to the people of the nation it served. In the secret archives of the Intelligence he was listed as James Christopher, but he was content that his civilian name remain unknown.

His blue eyes grew dark with apprehension as he saw an officer hurry from the operations-office toward Major Masson. He was a trim, erect figure in his flying suit. His clean-cut face indicated at a glance that he was American to the core. Because he profoundly appreciated the importance of these air maneuvers, and realized the demoralizing effect the delay must have on the waiting millions, he followed the officer to Major Masson's side.

"Colonel Parsons is on the wire, sir, speaking from Jay Field, Governors Island. He reminds us that he is to take off immediately we are in the air. He cannot fly until we are under way, sir. He is demanding an explanation and—"

Masson snapped: "He knows damned well I can't give flight orders until the unit from Mitchell Field is in the air. I'm being kept grounded because they haven't yet appeared. I can't do anything but wait. What the devil's the matter with them over there? Can't you get them on the line?"

Operator 5 listened intently as a second officer hurried from the operations office. "It's no good trying to raise Mitch-

ell Field, sir. There is no answer on the phone. I've tried to get them by wireless, but that's hopeless too. There's no way—"

"What?" Masson queried sharply.

"Why can't you get an answer from Mitchell? There are hundreds of men on that field. The biggest air-unit of the metropolitan area is detailed there. You're talking nonsense!"

"I can't explain it, sir," the second officer answered doggedly, "but it's true."

The major again scanned the empty sky. "I don't understand a damned bit of this. Almost half an hour has passed and there's not a single unit following orders. Lieutenant Weigall! Fly over to Mitchell Field at once. Find out why the devil—"

Masson broke off as a third officer came to a breathless stop facing him.

"Major-General Falk is calling from New York City, sir. His orders are to disregard all previous instructions, and fly at once. We are to circle over New York, then proceed northward along the coast. Apparently, sir, he has been able to reach only a few fields near here. He has issued them all the same orders." Major Masson exploded. "Months of planning, and now it's all gone for nothing! I've slaved on these plans, and the whole thing's shot to pieces. Signal ready to take off!"

THE RELAYED orders flashed across the field as Major

Masson turned to his plane. Operator 5, still remaining at the commander's side, saw the pilots stiffen in their pits. The speeding propellers blew a tearing wind across the tarmac. The metallic drone grew into a thunderous roar as Major Masson turned sharp eyes on Operator 5.

"Are you here because you suspected something like this might happen?"

Jimmy Christopher answered cryptically: "I am not very surprised, major."

"What?" Masson glared. "You expected all these careful plans to be disrupted? Did you warn General Staff? Did you tell them that this delay will panic those who trusted—?"

"General Staff has my complete information," Operator 5 answered quietly. "There was no course but to continue with the plans. We know only that every one of our defense units has been under close observation by members of an unidentified, subversive organization."

Masson gestured angrily. "What must those millions of people be thinking? They've been told that they have an air force second to none. They were promised protection against any attacker. 'Our air corps can be marshaled within a few minutes to repulse any invader'—that sort of stuff! Now we aren't even able to stage a simple demonstration-flight after months of the most careful planning. They can't be blamed for thinking we'd be helpless in case of an actual attack! Damned if they can!"

Major Masson climbed angrily into the pit of his plane. Operator 5 ran to the edge of the field as the roar of the scores of hot engines became a deafening thunder. The cyclone caused by the propellers sent sand flying as the pilots tensed to follow the take-off order. Jimmy Christopher was at the side of his pursuit ship when Masson flashed the signal.

Quickly, the rows of gleaming wings bent in the middle. The crates sped across the field, tails lifting, forming a V as they launched into the air. A second formation, and a third, sped into a swift climb while the commanding officer led the way. Operator 5 climbed to his own office and watched as the trim formations began to sweep across the Bay. They banked smoothly—the first move in a majestic wheel which would swing them directly over Manhattan Island—and as they swerved, a second bevy of battle birds zoomed into the air from Governors Island.

Jimmy Christopher's motor sang smoothly as he opened the throttle. He roared across an almost deserted field. A swift, even climb sent him winging across dark-blue water. He circled once, allowing time for the Governors Island unit to fall into line, before he dressed his ship to follow.

The inspiring series of V formations straightened. The two units blended into a parade winding its way toward the heart of New York. Operator 5 flew at some distance from them, watching intently, while they coursed smoothly above the Bay. He felt a strange premonition of disaster as he followed. The gleaming wings, formed in beautiful array under the brilliant sun, seemed somehow—he felt an eerie chill striking at his heart—doomed!

And suddenly, silently, without the slightest warning, doom struck!

The first hint of it was a strange, dark glow that filtered through the air in which the V-formations were sailing. The atmosphere abruptly changed to a brilliant violet. A clean-cut shaft appeared striking straight down from the zenith. It was as though a gigantic searchlight, poised in cosmic space, had shot a purplish beam directly toward the core of the earth. The color flashed over the glistening wings of the armada for one brief second, then vanished again.

DURING THAT fleeting instant, Operator 5 followed it with his eyes. He glimpsed the color gleaming on the water of the Bay, bathing over a freighter which was plowing sturdily through the swells. He saw the violet shaft rising as far into the heavens as his sight could reach. It was like a motionless, silent bolt of dazzling lightning during its amazingly short existence.

Mystified, frozen by a nameless dread, Jimmy Christopher threw his plane into a bank even while he peered at the roaring formations. His apprehension increased as he sensed a change come over the speeding wings. At first it was a mere looseness in the formations. The almost unnoticeable raggedness increased, as several ships drifted from their positions—until at last, the smart, straight lines were hopelessly broken.

In a moment, every crate was swinging erratically, weaving from side to side, bucking up and down, as though battled by a terrific wind. Then, as the strange effect of the violet beam continued its mysterious work, the formations disintegrated, and planes began to plunge!

Two crates sideswiped, began to spill downward, wing whirling over broken wing. One pulled into a tight zoom, then slipped into a vicious spin. Others sagged from their flight level toward the Bay and certain destruction. Again and again, the crash of collisions broke through the drone of the dying motors. Shattered crates rained earthward. Operator 5 stared in cold horror while havoc swept the battle birds from the sky.

Flames whipped back over planes locked together in an embrace of death. Spinning crates drove toward the dark waters with power plants screaming banshee wails. Others dropped their noses and dived with full open throttles into the Bay. Each, after a smashing impact, became sinking wreckage in which dead men were hopelessly entangled. One after another, destruction knocked the planes from the air until, at the end of a few swift minutes, no crate remained aloft.

Jimmy Christopher snapped the switch of his short-wave radio transmitter while he peered aghast at the littered surface of the Bay. The tramp steamer was plunging now across a watery graveyard. Its speed did not slacken, nor did it launch any boats as its prow ploughed through swells filled with fragments of the destroyed planes. The sea was a heaving blanket of stark disaster when Operator 5 called sharply into the microphone: "MW! Signaling MW!"

The answer flashed from the air: "MW on your wave."

"Operator 5 calling. Bring Z-7 to the microphone!"

The voice that followed was deep and chesty, that of the man who commanded the world-wide activities of the United States Intelligence. He was nameless, even to his most trusted undercover agents. He was shrewd, tireless, unstintingly devoted to protecting the United States against subversive forces and the dangerous activities of foreign espionage agents. Operator 5's amazing information—that the eastern army air-fields were being secretly watched by an unknown organization—had brought him to the secret Manhattan headquarters of the Intelligence. His driving tones carried clearly through the ether:

"Operator 5! What the devil's happened to the planes? I saw them fall! The whole General Staff witnessed the disaster. You viewed it at close quarters. What's your report?"

Jimmy Christopher answered tightly: "I'm at a dead loss, Chief. Every plane of the Miller and Governors Island units has been destroyed. Whatever hit them is a complete mystery. The bodies of the dead pilots must be recovered, if possible, for autopsies. That may give us a clue, but we can't hope for much. What about the other units, Chief?"

Z-7's voice crackled. "They haven't even taken off. Major-General Falk has been trying to reach those fields by telephone and radio, but he hasn't been able to raise them. We don't know what the devil has happened. Our entire air-display is hopelessly destroyed."

JIMMY CHRISTOPHER threw his plane into a sharp bank as he answered. "I'm heading for Mitchell Field now, Chief. I'll investigate conditions there and report. Before I sign off—has there been any report from Tim Donovan?"

"We've heard nothing from him. Get word to us from Mitchell as soon as possible, Operator 5!"

Jimmy Christopher sent his swift pursuit ship driving at top speed toward the famous army air-field at Mineola, Long Island. Circling above it, he peered down at a bewildering sight. Scores of battle planes were drawn up in perfect alignment across the tarmac, ready for the take-off. Their propellers were flashing

JIMMY CHRISTOPHER

over; pilots were seated in their cubbyholes. Near the operations-building, officers were standing in small groups. Abruptly, Operator 5 sensed something strange in the scene, and again felt a dread presentiment of danger as he nosed down for a landing.

His plane trundled over the smooth sand to a position near the offices. The motors of the other crates were giving out a steady drone when he braked and climbed from the pit. Gazing around curiously, he strode briskly to an officer he recognized—Major Langland, who had been detailed to lead the Mitchell Field units in the great air-display. Four other officers were standing at Langland's side, and the major was looking intently at his watch. None of the men gave Operator 5 a glance as he paused to say:

"Sir, General Staff has been trying to reach this field in order to learn—"

Jimmy Christopher's words faded on his cold lips. Still Major Langland had not moved! The men around him were likewise staring at the watch ticking in his hand, but none of them gave the slightest response. They stood immobile as statues as Jimmy Christopher searched their pale faces. He stepped back, a gasp of amazement rising from his dry throat, stunned by a sudden realization.

Like figures in a waxworks, the officers remained motionless while Operator 5 stared at the pilots in the pits of the humming planes. The hand of the nearest aviator, holding a bar of chocolate, was raised to the man's mouth—but it did not move!

Another was leaning across the cowling, smiling, lips half-open as if to shout—but he uttered no word. The man in the crate beyond was laughing—but there was no sound at all! In shocked dismay, Jimmy Christopher realized that each of the pilots was frozen statue-like, just as the officers standing near the point ship were!

Operator 5 hurried across the field. He saw scores of automobiles standing on the roads flanking it. Fumes pouring from the exhausts showed that the motors were running, but not a wheel was turning. Inside them men, women and children maintained fixed positions. At the intersection, a traffic policeman was standing with both hands upraised, a whistle in his teeth. He made not the slightest movement as Operator 5 stared.

His soul-chilling astonishment growing, Jimmy Christopher surveyed the hundreds of men and women crowding against the high, mesh fence encircling the field. He saw them in the act of speaking to one another, stooping, turning, laughing—but not one of them moved! In the lips of the nearest man, a cigarette had burned away, leaving the scar of a burn—but in his set expression, there was not the slightest suggestion of pain! Driven by increasing anxiety, Operator 5 ran toward the operations-offices.

At the point ship, Major Langland and his fellow officers were still gazing at the ticking watch. Inside of the door, Jimmy Christopher discovered the same uncanny state of suspended activity. He saw an officer sitting at a desk in the act of writing, a word half finished under his poised pen. He saw another man frozen in the very act of opening the drawer of a file cabinet.

At the radio panels, operators sat stolidly, ignoring the buzzing in phones pressed to their ears. At the telephone switchboard, another lieutenant sat, oblivious to the flashing red signal-lights before his wide-open, glazed eyes.

Operator 5 peered around, his heart beating cold. Nowhere on the famous field was there the slightest movement except the spinning propellers. Nowhere was there the sound of a voice—merely the steady drone of the motors.

In numb dismay, Jimmy Christopher realized the dread truth. Every person on and near the field—pilots, officers and spectators alike, the scores in the motionless cars and the hundreds crowding along the fences—every one of them had been struck by a paralytic, instantaneous death...!

CHAPTER 2
SECRET OF THE WILDERNESS

S ECRET INTELLIGENCE headquarters MW, in Manhattan, was located on the top floor of one of the tallest structures in the metropolis. It was reached by a special elevator, accessible only to those uttering a closely guarded code-word. It was the focus of a web of special wires which bound it to WDC-13, the central office of the service, in Washington, and kept it in touch with its undercover activities all over the United States.

In the busy rooms, doubly guarded by alert sentinels and its lofty situation, Intelligence men labored to protect the nation against destructive influences and the hidden work of foreign spies. Clattering teletype machines continually exchanged vital reports with operatives in the field. Short-wave equipment, tremendously sensitive and powerful—connecting with secret offices in foreign countries—functioned constantly. Here was maintained a duplicate of the largest and most complete finger-print file in the world, that in WDC-13. In its laboratories, every known device for the scientific investigation of crime was available. MW was a vital unit in the most efficient and modern detective system in the world.

And tonight, behind closely guarded doors, a meeting of national importance was being held....

Operator 5 faced eight grave men across a shining confer-ence table. The black-eyed man garbed in gray, to whom he addressed his report, was Z-7. The others were the most import-ant members of the joint board of the United States Army and navy. Following Jimmy Christopher's amazing telephonic report from Mitchell Field, they had waited with grim impatience for his appearance. Now he stood erect and square-shouldered before them, his clear eyes reflecting the dread he felt, as he said:

"One thing is certain, gentlemen. Mitchell Field was turned into a graveyard by the same strange force that knocked the Miller and Governors Island flights from the sky."

Z-7 added tensely: "I have a report here concerning the bodies of the pilots recovered from the Bay. Each was found in a condition like *rigor mortis*. Each died in exactly the same way, and apparently, instantly. But there is absolutely no indication of what killed them. Operator 5, have you any clue to the identity of the force which struck them down?"

"I have not," Jimmy Christopher admitted. "It's an entirely new power. I am fairly well informed on similar forces created in the laboratory, but the violet beam resembles none of them. Its source is even more mysterious. I saw it strike straight down, you will recall, apparently from a tremendous height."

Major-General Falk, Chief of Staff, asked tersely: "Is it possible the beam came from some craft flying at a great elevation—possibly from the stratosphere?"

"It is possible," Jimmy Christopher agreed. "We will investigate. Yet the terrific power of the beam must be required to generate it. It lasted only a second, but it was forceful enough to kill every man it touched instantly."

Brigadier-General Braxton, Assistant Chief of Staff, War Plans Division, rapped the table sharply. "Whatever this power is, it was turned on our planes deliberately—with the purpose of wrecking our maneuvers. It succeeded completely!" Eyes glinting, he turned to the others. "How the devil can we fight this force if we don't know what it is?"

GENERAL FALK glowered. "It has already panicked the nation. The maneuvers were intended to reassure them, but instead, our failure has filled their hearts with fear. Such events as this, gentlemen, lead to insurrection. Somehow, we've got to redeem ourselves."

Operator 5 said quietly: "I think you may expect the power to strike again!"

They all peered at him in dismay. He studied their drawn faces during a moment of anxious silence. Z-7 rose tensely, holding a pack of yellow flimsies in one hand. He spread them on the table with a gesture of despair.

"Operator 5, I withheld this information from you until you reported. You are not yet fully aware of the widespread havoc we've already suffered. You saw scores of planes knocked from the sky; you found a field peopled with dead—yet that is only a small part of the disaster. These telegrams tell us that the same force struck no less than twelve times—in twelve different places—this afternoon!"

Jimmy Christopher's face paled.

"One after another, our air units were hit. It spread wild destruction up and down the coast, and inland. Each time, it left an Army post or an air-field with no animate thing left. If what you say is true—if the force strikes again—our defenses are completely at the hidden enemy's mercy."

"Even that is not all!" General Falk blurted. "This afternoon, a freighter putting in from Rio was following a course in the Bay directly beneath the Miller and Governors Island units. Coast Guard boats, going after the fallen men, found that every living thing on it had perished. The violet beam had struck it and turned it into an argosy of the dead!"

Rear-Admiral Seagrave spoke rushingly: "Think what it will mean if that damnable weapon is turned upon our cities! The beam penetrated the steel decks of the freighter—that means it can strike through roofs and walls. It is capable of destroying all life it touches. In a few seconds, it can make New York a city of corpses."

Brigadier-General Braxton asked tensely: "Operator 5, your report to Z-7 was the first hint that destructive plans were being formulated against us. Who is behind this devilish attack?"

Operator 5 answered grimly: "That, gentlemen, I intend to learn, if Z-7's orders permit it. So far I have acted only on suspicion that a closely knit, secret organization is at work. I trailed certain men known to be dangerous revolutionists. I found them purchasing photographic maps, and spying upon the army posts around New York City. I searched the room of one named Gerard Apito during his absence, and found the locations of the fields annotated on the maps. Feeling certain some destructive purpose lay behind this espionage activity—"

"Did you arrest him?" General Braxton demanded quickly.

Before Operator 5 could answer, a sharp knock sounded on the door. Z-7 strode to it at once and drew the bolt. An Intelligence man from the communications-room spoke quickly through the crack.

"Long distance call for Operator 5!"

"CONNECT IT with this instrument," Jimmy Christopher directed. He answered General Braxton as he moved toward the phone: "I did not arrest Apito, because he could have told me very little. Instead, I shadowed him, hoping that he might unwittingly reveal the identity of the leader he serves. Because I wished to watch other developments today, I put my friend, Tim Donovan, on the job of shadowing him. The fact that I've had no report from Tim means that—"

Lifting the receiver, Operator 5 heard a breathless voice rush over the line: "Jimmy! I'm on the job!"

Braxton snapped: "You actually entrusted that important task to a mere boy? It's preposterous!"

Jimmy Christopher whispered into the transmitter: "Hold it a moment, old timer." His blue eyes narrowed at Braxton. "Tim Donovan," he answered levelly, "is as skilled a shadower as any agent in the Intelligence, General. I have every confidence in him. And he is reporting right now!" As Braxton scowled, Operator 5 smiled tightly and spoke into the transmitter again: "Go ahead, Tim."

"Jimmy!" The boy spoke swiftly. "I'm calling from a Forest Ranger station in Eastern Pennsylvania. Its due North of Worden. I followed Apito here by car. He arrived after dark, went straight to a place hidden in the hills. Every path leading to it is guarded, so I haven't been able to find out what it is. Other men have been following him in. It must mean that there's some kind of a secret meeting being held here tonight."

"Good work, Tim!" Jimmy Christopher exclaimed. "Listen carefully: I'm leaving at once by gyro. Find a safe position near the secret meeting place and watch. In ninety minutes, begin flashing your light into the sky. I'll spot it and come down. We'll look into that hideaway together. Okay, Tim?"

"Right, Jimmy!"

Operator 5's smile persisted as he lowered the instrument and again faced the officers of the General Staff.

"One further point, gentlemen," he said firmly, "must be brought out. It's true we've been attacked by a ghastly power. We know now that its purpose is to disrupt, if not totally destroy, our defenses. And it's obvious that the enemy has at least one agent who is thoroughly familiar with the detailed Army plans."

Major-General Falk stared aghast. "What are you saying?" he blurted. "Are you insinuating that some high officer in command has betrayed his country?"

Operator 5 leaned forward tensely, his eyes glinting. "I am insinuating nothing, General Falk. I am bluntly stating a fact. Someone in the army command—perhaps a member of this joint board—aided the attack on us this afternoon, if he did not actually direct it."

Z-7 exclaimed: "That's a very serious charge, Operator 5!"

"And you'll have to prove it!" General Falk snapped.

"I'll do so, gladly, and now. Consider the situation, gentlemen. The force struck at the precise moment its demoralizing effect would be the greatest. It was directed by one who knew exactly where each unit was stationed, when each flight was due to take off, just which fields must be hit in order to disrupt the whole program. No one outside the army command can get that information. The inevitable conclusion is that one of the officers who helped plan the maneuvers also helped to destroy them!"

Z-7 peered appalled at the yellow flimsies on the table. "It must be true! The locations of the fields which sent in these reports—they show it! No one not thoroughly familiar with every detail of the maneuvers could have planned it. That's treason!"

Operator 5 turned briskly to the door, opened it. Pausing, he studied the faces of the officers who held the highest positions attainable in the army and navy. He said calmly: "The guilty man must necessarily consider himself bound by a greater allegiance than loyalty to the United States. He is among you. It is my duty, gentlemen, to identify him—and to destroy him!"

Quietly he stepped from the room of silence....

BLACK WINGS soared through the black sky that shrouded the rugged hills of Eastern Pennsylvania. The bat-like craft circled slowly, its engine muffled. At times it poised almost motionless in the night. It was an autogyro of the most modern design. Operator 5 peered over its cowling into a baffling wilderness of darkness.

He had sped in his Diesel-engined roadster from Headquarters MW to the little wharf house—at the end of a bleak street on the East Side of Manhattan—where he kept the craft secretly hangared. After carefully plotting his course toward the source of Tim Donovan's long distance call, he had launched into the sky from a room provided with a retractable roof. The night sheen of New York had swiftly receded. Flying by instrument, Jimmy Christopher had winged into an almost trackless region. Now, while the lights of the town of Worden glimmered below him, he switched off his beacons and searched the vast expanse of the heavens.

He sensed another presence in the air. As he hovered, he became certain his craft was not alone in the sky. A muted droning carried on the wind and grew louder. He glimpsed the faint outlines of a plane shuttling downward without lights. Quickly he brought a pair of powerful binoculars to his eyes and followed the floating shadow. Sharp surprise filled him when he saw, by the dim silver glow of the stars, that it was marked by the tricolored cocarde of the United States Army!

The plane stayed a moment in his vision, then vanished in the thick gloom below. Jimmy Christopher had had no opportunity to recognize the goggled pilot. He kept his craft hovering while he listened to the soughing of the plane's motor. The fact that it was descending into an unlighted field, without even the aid of its wing-lamps, convinced him that the man at the controls was a skilled aviator. The pulsing of the power-plant continued several long minutes, then whispered away into the brooding silence. The plane was down.

Jimmy Christopher's binoculars could not penetrate the jungle gloom that lay over the rolling hills. The rugged region which spread below him was almost untouched by civilization. It was a wilderness which had scarcely changed since the settlement of the original American colonies. Yet Tim Donovan had reported trailing a suspect into the black fastnesses of this remote country. Somewhere below, Operator 5 knew, the boy was waiting now.

Anxious minutes passed until he caught the first brief flash of the light signal. It was a bright spot that gleamed three times, then disappeared. It came again as Operator 5 swung the gyro toward it. He descended cautiously, knowing that he might very easily wreck the craft—that a sharp crag might tear off a wing, or thick trees trap him in tentacle-like branches so that he could not rise again. Chancing, too, that the sound of his motor might spread an alarm, he drifted within a few yards of the spot where the light shone.

An eager voice called upward. "Straight down! It's a level, open spot! All safe, Jimmy!"

Operator 5 dropped the remaining short distance. The craft bounded on its fat tires as he cut the motor. While he climbed out, a boy rushed toward him. Tim Donovan gripped Jimmy Christopher's hand warmly.

★ ★ TIM DONOVAN ★ ★

"Gee, I'm glad to see you!" the youngster whispered. "I've been on the job every minute!"

OPERATOR 5 smiled admiringly as he studied Tim's face in the dim starlight. Nothing save death could ever break the bond of affection which bound him to this tough Irish lad. Since that drenching night on the lower East Side, more than two years ago, when Tim Donovan had saved Jimmy Christopher from a killer's bullet, they had been inseparable. The boy had aided him loyally in many important and dangerous cases. As Operator 5's unofficial assistant—his credential was the mystic skull ring which Jimmy Christopher had presented to him—he had repeatedly proved his courage and skill.

Tonight his face was drawn with hunger and fatigue. The thorns and twigs of the wilderness had torn his clothing. In spite of the hardships, he had stuck to the trail assigned him by Jimmy Christopher. He forgot his discomfort, and grinned broadly, as Operator 5 proudly returned his grip. "I knew I could depend on you, Tim."

"Jimmy, other men have come up into the hills and followed the trail Apito took," the boy reported. "I've counted ten since I phoned you. I've found only one way of getting into that region, and it's guarded. I didn't try to get in because, if I happened to get caught, I wouldn't be able to signal you down. What's the next move?"

"You were right, Tim," Operator 5 answered thoughtfully. "There is some kind of secret meeting being held. But why this remote region, and what's behind the plan? You and I are going to find out, old timer."

"Okay, Jimmy!" the boy whispered eagerly. "I'll show you the trail."

The boy cautiously led the way down a steep slope. His moves were as quick and silent as those of a wild animal. Operator 5 followed him to the edge of a winding road. When they were sure the way was clear, they quickly crossed. Once in the shadow of the thick trees, the boy pointed out a cleared space, screened from the road, in which a number of cars were parked. Tim moved warily to a narrow footpath which twisted between the

trees, and gestured that this was the guarded trail which Apito had taken to the secret meeting-place.

Operator 5 advanced slowly, every sense sharp. He felt presences lurking in the gloom along the path, but he advanced with even, silent tread. Tim Donovan kept close at his heels. A faint rustle of leaves warned that someone, hidden by the darkness, was watching at a point directly ahead. Jimmy Christopher took slow strides toward the invisible danger. Expecting a sudden attack any moment, he held himself ready....

It came swiftly. A black figure leaped from the shelter of a tree trunk, directly onto the trail. Upraised arms swung a heavy cudgel with baffling speed. The murderous weapon was slashing toward Jimmy Christopher's head when he leaped aside. It descended with vicious power, past his shoulder, as he struck out. His stiffened fingers moved like lightning to the neck of the black assailant.

Operator 5's hand twisted at the instant of impact. The points of his fingers drove with paralyzing force to a vital nerve-center in the attacker's throat. The jiu-jitsu blow resulted in an explosion of breath and instantly, the other man's body became rigid. He poised, the cudgel trailing on the ground. His eyes stared wildly in the starlight as he toppled to the trail-side like a statue pushed from its base.

Bending quickly, Operator 5 made sure that the effects of his counter-attack would keep the guardian of the secret trail unconscious fully an hour. He straightened, eyes slitted, and resumed his descent. Tim Donovan kept anxiously at his side while they advanced through bewildering, threatening darkness.

A SECOND attack struck even more suddenly than the first. Jimmy Christopher sprang ahead as a sharp, slashing sound cut the air. He whirled in dismay as a stifled gasp broke from Tim Donovan. He saw the boy squirming in a desperate attempt to escape the loop of a rope that had dropped from above. The taut strand was drawn around his throat. A savage pull jerked the agonized boy from his feet as Operator 5 lunged back.

Jimmy Christopher's hand darted to the buckle of his belt. The clasp was now revealed as the hilt of a rapier sheathed in the narrow leather band encircling his waist. Operator 5 whipped the blade of supple Toledo steel so swiftly it became a twinkling streak in the starlight. Its razor-sharp edge slashed against the strand from which the frantic Irish lad was dangling. Tim Donovan sprawled down, gasping, as the rope parted.

A savage snarl came from the darkness among the branches as Jimmy Christopher gripped the severed end. He jerked on the rope with all his strength. Another snarl of rage cut the air as a dark figure spilled down from the limb. A heavy-set man sprang up while Operator 5 stood with rapier poised. The needle-point of the blade poised above the attacker's heart as Jimmy Christopher warned:

"Stand where you are!"

Fanatical eyes glared at Operator 5 while the big man

crouched. Unreasoning foolhardiness threw the sentry into a leap, fingers clawing for Jimmy Christopher's throat. Though Operator 5 made no move, a tremor passed through the rapier. The big man jerked to a stop, staring down in amazement at the bright line of steel piercing his chest. He hung on toe-tips an instant, then dropped. As he rolled on the trail, Jimmy Christopher's blade glittered red.

Tim Donovan tore the choking noose from his neck. Peering down at the face of the man in the shadow, he gasped: "He did that to himself, Jimmy! It wouldn't have happened if he'd obeyed your warning."

Operator 5 answered grimly: "I couldn't use a gun, because the report would bring them all down on us. There's a secret in this place that's being desperately guarded, Tim. We're close to it now. Stick with me, old timer."

His rapier was again sheathed and coiled about his slender waist when he continued along the trail with the anxious boy. The serpentine path wound through jungle-thick growths. An oppressive silence pervaded the hills. Operator 5 and Tim Donovan advanced with the utmost caution until, abruptly, they rounded a bend that revealed a great, cleared space.

It lay low in the darkness pooled between the rearing humps of the hills. They paused in the flooding gloom, gazing at the dim outlines of two buildings. The nearest was a squat structure with blinded windows. Farther back, in the center of the clearing, the second loomed inside a high, mesh fence. The air pulsed faintly, and Operator 5 deduced that a great power-plant was in action. Not the slightest gleam of light shone from either of the two structures concealed in the wilderness.

Operator 5 remained motionless a moment, making sure he was not observed. He felt certain that other sentries were posted around the fringe of the clearing, but there was not the slightest flutter of movement to betray their presence. He knew that to reach the buildings would mean risking passage through the clearing—an even greater danger than the guarded trail—but, eyes and ears alert, he resumed his advance.

ONCE IN the clear, he circled quickly to the building enclosed in the wire fence. When he paused in the shadow, a faint whirring and crackling sound indicated that powerful generators were functioning. Jimmy Christopher brought his lips close to Tim Donovan's ear and whispered:

"I'm going to try to discover the purpose of this power-plant, Tim. I've another special job for you. Over there, near the edge of a clearing, there's a plane sitting. Do you see it?"

The boy's gaze followed Jimmy Christopher's pointing finger. With difficulty he discerned a faint shine of wings in the gloom. The plane which Operator 5 had heard descend was crouched in the open, turned ready for a take-off.

"Watch it, Tim," he directed. "I want to find out, if possible, who brought it here. The pilot may come back to it soon. Learn his identity if you can."

"Okay, Jimmy!" the boy answered quietly. "I'll find out who he is!"

Operator 5 waited anxiously while Tim Donovan stole across the open. He vanished in the gloom. Allowing him time to take a position near the plane, Jimmy Christopher turned alertly to the mesh fence. Following it, he found a gate that was securely locked. Though he possessed skeleton keys which could easily open it, a sixth sense warned him not to bring them into use because an electrical alarm would signal the yielding of the gate. He circled back into the shadow, fastened his hands firmly in the meshes, and began to climb....

His heart speeded as the fence creaked under his weight. When he reached the top, he balanced and listened. He realized that, once he entered the enclosed space, he would be inside a trap which would cost him his life if he were discovered. Lips grimly pressed, he dropped to the ground.

He glided to the side of the building. Its windows were so closely blinded no light shone out. As he drifted along the wall, he found iron ladder rungs cleated near a corner. Puzzled, he pulled himself up and gazed across the flat roof. Lines of light, shining through narrow cracks, drew him close.

He saw that he was standing on a broad panel which could be withdrawn on rollers to expose the room below. The chinks of light gleamed at its edges. While the building vibrated with the hum of the generators, Operator 5 pressed his eye to one of the slits. Brilliant globes burning below him revealed an astounding scene. The center of the deep room was occupied by a gigantic parabolic reflector. The grayish tinge of its polished surface revealed that it was molded of lead. At its focal point, a huge discharge tube was affixed. Jimmy Christopher recognized it as a cathode projector capable of sending out a powerful penetrating beam. Yet he was puzzled by the fact that the reflector was directed straight upward, and that it was apparently incapable of swinging to a horizontal level.

He carefully studied the mechanism on which the great reflector was mounted. A system of wheels, shafts and worm gears was provided for altering the angle of its projection, but only to the extent of a few degrees. At whatever point it was directed, within the limit of its adjustments, it must shoot its beam high into the sky. Operator 5 made sure of the fact, but his certainty only increased his bewilderment as to the function of the massive device.

It could not possibly be the direct means of attack which had been turned on the United States defenses, he knew, because it was totally impossible to turn its invisible shaft upon the point at which the power had struck.

MEN IN coveralls were at work in the room. Some were checking the readings of meters on a great, black panel. Others were working at desks, consulting maps, making notations, manipulating slide rules. That plans were being formulated even now, for some strange use of the mysterious projector, Jimmy Christopher could not doubt.

He drew back cautiously, and descended the rungs affixed to the wall. He crossed the open yard without a sound, and again climbed the high, mesh fence. Making sure he was not being watched, he hurried through the gloom toward the other building. He paused at a wall, listening intently, and sensed movements beyond it. Men were speaking inside, but their low tones made their words unintelligible. Within this structure, Jimmy Christopher surmised the dread, secret meeting was in progress.

He stole silently to a door. When he twisted the knob, it yielded. Peering along a dark corridor, he brought his automatic from its armpit holster. He stepped in alertly, closed the door behind him. The voices were clearer. Operator 5 took soundless steps along the hall, toward a heavily draped doorway which connected with the hidden meeting-room.

He scarcely breathed as he bent close to the drawn curtains. As he parted them a fraction of an inch, with the utmost care, a cold, precise voice spoke within the room beyond.

"Comrades of the Secret Loyalists! The blow we struck against the so-called United States today is the mighty culmination of more than one hundred and fifty years of ardent endeavor. We have begun to wipe out the perfidy of Cornwallis. This land will again become the colony of Mother England. Long live the King!"

Astonishment filled Operator 5 as he peered into the room beyond the draped door. A score of men were standing in file, facing the speaker. Black hoods covered their faces. On the black robes which enveloped them, gleaming brilliants formed a design. It was a royal crown. They stood at attention, their eyes glittering through the slits of their masks, at the man who was addressing them.

He was an even more astounding figure. His garb was a brightly colored uniform. His long, red coat with its regimental facings, his gray broad-brimmed hat and gray breeches, his glittering sword, all bespoke a century which had passed. A black mask covered his face, giving startling contrast to the whiteness of his wig. His was the uniform of a high-ranking British officer at the time of the American Revolution!

He spoke ringingly: "Our work goes on, comrades of the Secret Loyalists! Tomorrow, at high noon, we strike again, to destroy the officers at the rebel army headquarters for the area of New York. Step by step we will crush these revolutionist colonies until at last they will be left utterly defenseless. The long-lived work of Major Brennock, first leader of the Secret Loyalists, will achieve triumph at last in the name of the King!"

The uniformed man flashed his sword into the air. His robed lieutenants snapped smart salutes. The gesture was to bring an end to the amazing meeting—but a sudden interruption came.

Operator 5 whirled from the curtains in chilled dismay as the door at the end of the corridor swung open.

CHAPTER 3
STRATOSPHERE SEARCH

B REATH CAUGHT, Jimmy Christopher shrank against the black wall. He slid along it swiftly as dark figures crowded into the corridor. He gripped the knob of a door, opened it on darkness, and slipped through. Automatic in hand, he peered back at the man who charged toward the curtains. The first jerked it aside and stood defiantly erect in the light.

In bewilderment, Operator 5 saw that this man was a double of the uniformed leader in the room. He wore the same red-and-gray military garb of the time of the American rebellion. His sharp, green eyes glittered dangerously through his black mask. He gripped his sword, stepped aside alertly, and uttered a rasping command:

"Seize the traitor!"

Startled and puzzled, Operator 5 watched. The men who hurried into the meeting room were robed in black, and 28 wore the same insignia of the Diamond Crown. With guns glittering in their gloved hands, they swarmed upon the masked officer who had addressed the secret assembly. He drew his sword desperately, but as he raised it, the raiders seized his arms. They forced him against the wall, pinioning him by wrists and throat. His double advanced with slow, deliberate stride, smiling with evil triumph.

"The cause of the Secret Loyalists," the second uniformed man declared pompously, "is greater than the lineage of its leader. We have learned of your treachery to the cause. You will suffer the penalty of death."

The man at the wall straightened coldly. "You charge me with a lie. You cannot question my loyalty. I have inherited my patriotism from the creator of the Secret Loyalists. You are guilty of treason, not I!"

The masked officer facing him laughed tauntingly. "You have not only been charged with betraying the cause. You have been

Desperately, Tim grabbed
the wheel and was instantly
dragged from the ground!

tried in secret, and found guilty. You are no longer our leader, no longer one of us. Loyalists! You have your orders!"

Peering through the door, Operator 5 saw that the seized man stood alone against the robed members of the secret band. Obeying the command of the second masked officer, they dragged him from the wall. They ripped away the golden buttons and the facings from his red tunic, and tore it off him. Holding him helpless, they whipped ropes around his ankles and wrists. In spite of his efforts to escape, he was securely bound. He answered his accuser's mocking laugh with a firm, defiant stare.

"Take him away!"

Operator 5 watched the black-robed men force the bound officer out the door and along the hallway. As they passed outside, the masked commander laughed again. A gasp of dismay broke from Jimmy Christopher's lips when he saw the man turn to the door behind which he stood. He backed swiftly into the darkness, automatic leveled. Finger poised on the trigger, he eased along the wall.

The knob of the entrance was turning when his outstretched hand struck the frame of another door. He gripped the knob and swiftly stepped through as the entrance opened. The uniformed officer stood silhouetted on the sill when Operator 5 soundlessly closed his door. He retreated in thick darkness as a switch snapped in the other room, and steps sounded. They paused almost at once. Jimmy Christopher stood rigid, listening, during a moment of tight silence.

A rustle of papers told him that the masked man was working at a desk. He drew his fountain-pen torch from his pocket and touched the contact. The thin beam of light played upon a black panel to which electrical meters were affixed. Jimmy Christopher stepped toward it quickly, his eyes shining with elation. The apparatus he bent over, making a quick inspection, was a short-wave transmitter and receiver....

HIS HEART pounded as his mind sped. He threw a switch that brought a cherry-red glow to the vacuum tubes, then trimmed the oscillator. Sure that the equipment was functioning, he brought a microphone close to his lips. Again he heard a rustle of papers in the next room. Gun still in hand, he whispered:

"Calling MW. Calling MW."

He fitted phones to his ears and adjusted the receiving condensers to the exact point of MW's waveband. He felt sure the wireless impulses, radiating perhaps from an antenna concealed in the woods, was capable of reaching almost any point in the nation. Fearing that the radio operator might return to the room at any moment, he whispered his call again urgently: "MW! Operator 5 signaling MW!"

Movements were still audible in the adjoining room when an answering voice flashed through the ether.

"MW on your wave, Operator 5."

"Z-7, at once!"

Jimmy Christopher straightened in surprise as a sudden roar surged out of the night—the beating exhaust of an airplane motor. It told him the craft on the field—the Army plane he had discovered secretly descending to this hidden clearing— was going into action. The drone continued, blanketing all other sounds, while Operator 5 waited with burning nerves.

"Z-7 speaking," a voice said gruffly in the phones. "Where are you, Operator 5?"

"Chief!" Jimmy Christopher exclaimed. "I have a report and there is not a second to spare. Listen carefully. I am at the head-quarters of an organization called the Secret Loyalists, hidden in the hills near Worden, Pennsyl-vania. They directed the attack this afternoon. Tomorrow, at high noon, they will strike again—at

the army headquarters on Governors Island."

"What?"

"Order every available man to this place at once, Chief. It must be seized. There is a gigantic device here which may be the weapon of the new attack. Our best chance to escape another tragedy is to destroy it. If our attempt should fail, there are other preparations—"

Operator 5 paused, listening through the throaty note of the motor on the field. He could hear no sound now in the adjoining room. Holding his automatic ready, he watched the connecting door.

"Go on, Operator 5!"

"Other preparations, Chief. We can never hope to overcome

the death-force unless we learn its nature and source. We must provide for tests to be made on Governors Island at the zero hour tomorrow. Ask several government physicists to volunteer. They may be able to protect themselves by lining a room with lead sheeting. It's a gamble, Chief, but it must be taken.

"I will see that it's done."

"Another item, Chief. The army has a stratospheric balloon ready for a flight now. It must be put to use tomorrow, early enough so that it can reach the upper limits of the atmosphere at high noon. If I can return in time, I want to make that ascent myself. It will show once and for all whether the death ray is projected by some super-craft in the air."

"The balloon will be ready, Operator 5."

Operator 5 spun as a snap came from the connecting door. It flashed open as he faced it. With swift agility, a silhouetted figure sprang through. A sharp click brought a blinding brilliance into the room. Jimmy Christopher dropped the microphone and receivers as he retreated, eyes stinging. He was able to see only vaguely that the man who had entered was the masked leader in the strange military uniform.

THE CRACK of a shot shocked through the room. The bullet breathed coldly on Operator 5's cheek as he leveled his automatic. He fired once, aiming swiftly. A choking cry burst from the lips of the masked man as he sprang back with his gun-hand dripping red. His weapon spilled from his paralyzed fingers as be slapped the door shut.

Jimmy Christopher sprang to it and gripped the knob. A

stout bolt barred the way. He was whirling back when a hoarse shout penetrated the panels.

"Capture that spy!"

Operator 5 sped to a door at the opposite side of the room. He thrust through it into night darkness. As he turned to run along the wall, toward the front of the building, ghostly black figures appeared at the corner. Robed men, following the orders of their masked leader, rushed with guns glittering in their gloved fists. Jimmy Christopher darted back, then sprinted across the open into the sheltering shadows of the surrounding trees.

He crouched down, while the robed men scattered around the building in a swift search. His narrowed eyes glimpsed the appearance of another figure at the corner of the structure. The masked officer in historic British uniform snapped orders that sent still more robed men scurrying through the night. His green eyes glittered as he shouted:

"Kill that spy and evacuate the field!"

He went with quick strides in the direction of the waiting plane. Lights were flashing among the trees behind it. They revealed black figures moving swiftly, beating the bushes and probing into the shadows with their torches. Concern for Tim Donovan stung Operator 5's heart sharply as he heard a gruff shout:

"Somebody's hiding in here!"

"We saw him duck out of sight—a boy!"

The masked officer came to a stop beside the plane marked with the tricolored concentric circles of the United States Army. His rasping voice carried clearly to Jimmy Christopher:

"Find him and kill him!"

While Jimmy Christopher watched anxiously, the leader of the Secret Loyalists climbed to the controls of the plane. Behind it, robed men continued their search for Tim Donovan. The crown insignia on their black garments glittered brilliantly as they moved. Operator 5 rose and crept through the shadows toward the spot as the motor of the plane roared to a higher note.

Suddenly another shout: "There he is!"

The words were almost lost in the thunder of the airplane engine, but they brought Operator 5 to a chilled stop. A swift movement stirred the bushes near the edge of the clearing. Tim Donovan appeared, running swiftly. He sped into the open and plunged through the slipstream of the slashing propeller as lights flashed toward him. In terror, the boy whirled, seeking an avenue of escape, as the plane began to roll.

Black-robed men were rushing toward him from every direction. Glittering guns threatened him with blasting death as he broke into another sprint. The great tires of the plane were revolving as he threw himself toward the V-shaped truck braces. He gripped desperately with both hands, and was dragged from his feet instantly. The powerful motor of the plane pulled it swiftly to a faster speed. The flame of guns flashed toward the desperate boy as dust clouded over him.

JIMMY CHRISTOPHER stared in cold dismay. He knew that the boy was being pulled mercilessly across the ground, yet his frantic subterfuge had enabled him to escape his robed pursuers. His small fists were still gripped to the truck braces when the plane began to lift. Blood rushing, Operator 5 saw the boy dangling in mid air. Tim Donovan made a strenuous attempt to pull himself up while the wind tore at him. He was still hanging precariously when the blackness of the night curtained him from Operator 5's sight.

Jimmy Christopher realized in despair that a fall from the speeding plane would mean the death of the courageous lad. Even if he maintained his perch throughout the flight, he might be horribly crushed at the moment of landing. Helpless to aid the boy, Operator 5 retreated into the deeper blackness of the trees while the roar of the plane died into the gloom.

Robed men were still searching the area around the headquarters-building, and working through the woods. Operator 5 knew that to remain longer would mean certain capture. He sought his way through the thick gloom while other men in black hoods came rushing across the field. The voice of one carried clearly:

"Our orders are to evacuate the field! It is now known to the Intelligence. Three minutes to get away before the switch is thrown!"

The words sharpened Jimmy Christopher's alarm, though their exact meaning was lost to him. He hurried along the winding trail while lights flashed among the trees behind him. The search was spreading when he reached the road. He bounded across it, then climbed the steep slope toward the level area on which he had landed his gyro.

He was aware that the robed men were hastily leaving the secret field while he climbed to the controls. As he wrenched the crank, dread struck at his heart that the muffled beat of the engine might bring them in a murderous attack. The still-hot motor smoothed swiftly. Operator 5 tested it with the throttle, then threw off the brakes. The craft was rolling into its short take-off when he glimpsed phantom figures rushing up the slope toward him.

Flame flashed and bullets whined. Operator 5 answered with a fusillade that sent the black figures scattering for shelter. His singing engine pulled him with increasing speed across the flat while the horizontal vanes exerted their lifting power. As suddenly as a bird taking wing, the craft bounded up. A rattling fire sent slugs whistling around Jimmy Christopher as he soared.

He swerved sharply in the direction taken by the plane of the masked commander. The maneuver took him directly over the secret field. He was opening the throttle to its limit, determined to chase the other craft at top speed, when a cataclysmic force engulfed him....

An earth-shaking explosion shocked through the night without warning, from a point directly below the gyro. Blinding white flame geysered from broken ground. Clouds of thick fumes billowed into the air surrounding Operator 5. The terrific upheaval tore at his craft with savage violence. It rocked through the air crazily as earth rained down through the choking smoke. JIMMY CHRISTOPHER thrust desperately at his controls to rise clear, but a second tearing concussion followed swiftly. Peering down through the eye-stinging vapor, he saw the explosion strike through the building surrounded by the mesh fence. He realized that buried mines were being detonated electrically; that the robed men were obeying orders to destroy the field as they evacuated it. The ear-rending shocks came in quick, savage succession while Operator 5 fought to escape the turbulent air.

The controls of his careening craft were of no avail in the tempest created by the explosions. While he was tossed in the violent upheaval, the field was quaked again and again by the explosions. The buildings and all they contained became flying wreckage. Great, fuming pits opened. Suffocating vapors clouded high. The thunder of the shocks was echoed by a rumbling on the hillside as loose rocks spilled down in growing avalanches. The world became a chaotic turmoil through which Jimmy Christopher hopelessly struggled.

He thrust frantically at the controls as tearing winds flung him low over the trees. The branches became claws that clutched at his faltering wings. The gyro crashed into the jungle with a rending twist. Its wings ripped off as its fuselage plunged through. Operator 5 spilled from it into a darkness thicker than the night.

Rumbling echoes drummed in the distance and disappeared. The clouds of fumes dissolved in the wind. The field lay a black spread of destruction over which the silence of the wilderness reigned.

THE SWIFT pursuit plane passed across the black zenith like a winged ghost. Wind streamed over its cocarded wings and tore at the boy clinging to the V-brace of the trucks. Its relentless force threatened to tear him from his perilous position. Tim Donovan kept his grip on the tubes with a strength-draining effort as he peered, with speeding heart, down into the pit of the night.

With the lash of the wind beating upon him, while the plane was circling up from the field hidden in the wilderness, he had managed to pull himself to a higher position. Finding that the fat tire near him turned at the slightest touch, he was forced to support himself as best he could on the narrow braces. Each swerve of the plane, as the masked man in the pit touched the controls, threatened to throw him off into

space. Every moment of the flight had seemed an eternity of agony to the boy. Now, his whole body pulsing with fatigue, he looked down at the dark band of the Hudson River, and saw the glare of New York City loom on the horizon.

The plane banked sharply. Tim Donovan exerted all his waning strength to keep his hands closed on the tubes. The wind was a demoniacal fury striving mercilessly to pull him away. Teeth bared, eyes closed with the torture of his effort, the Irish lad managed to hold his position while the plane leveled. The note of its motor dropped to a lower tone as the craft began to glide.

New anxiety filled Tim Donovan's heart as he realized the pilot was preparing to land. The plane glided over a section north of the metropolis in which myriad lights twinkled. With motor cut, it continued to mush toward an area that lay like a black island in a glittering sea. Again the boy tightened his grip when the plane began to spiral. It screwed downward into thickening darkness, until a broad field blurred beneath the trucks.

Tim Donovan saw a huge house, then a low white structure squatting near the border of the spreading grounds. As the plane shuttled at an elevation of only a few feet, it passed the mansion. In front of the second building the boy glimpsed men in quick action. They opened wide doors, then hurried in the direction of the wavering craft. Tim strained back to escape the spinning tire as it touched.

His blood pounded when he realized that the plane was taxiing directly toward the white structure. If he remained on the brace, he was certain to be seen. A drop to the ground was a danger he was forced to risk. He lowered himself while the craft was still fifty yards from the yawning doors, then let go.

He struck with a shock that stunned him. He was only vaguely conscious of rolling over and over. His brain spun while he lay in dew-wet grass. As his senses cleared, he looked up alertly. The motor was no longer clicking over. The plane trundled to a stop at the side of the white building. The two men were hurrying toward it while the masked pilot climbed out.

Tim Donovan knew that he had not been seen, but now the broad grounds offered him no shelter. He sprang up and ran swayingly. He circled toward the side of the low building while he watched the men at the plane. The two in coveralls had climbed up and were lifting something heavy from the rear

50

cubby. The Irish lad came to a breathless stop at the side wall and saw them lower an unconscious man.

The mechanics lowered their bound prisoner to the ground. Immediately they bore against the wings of the pursuit, and wheeled it into the black space beyond the broad door. He heard them talking in low tones inside as he straightened at a new alarm. A car was approaching on the highway which ran alongside the estate, and the headlamps threw a brightening glare on him. He dropped breathless to the ground, peering up to watch the masked man in the red tunic.

WHILE TIM DONOVAN lay flat, the car passed. Darkness sheltered him again. He rose cautiously as the two mechanics hurried out of the disguised hangar. They strode to the bound captive as Tim carefully rounded the corner. He poised, then spurted through the open door. Quickly he retreated into the thick darkness. He crouched behind an oil drum in the rear corner.

He saw the two mechanics, about to lift the pinioned prisoner, stopped by a gruff command of the masked pilot.

"Take him into the house. I shall save him for a special death. Perhaps, when he strikes at the Atlantic Fleet, the day after tomorrow, he will himself be within range of the beam...! First, lock the hangar."

Tim Donovan's breath stopped as the two men in coveralls strode to the doors. The great panels slid quietly together on greased rollers. A lock clicked, then footfalls beat away. Tim groped anxiously to the door, and tugged at it with all his strength. He searched the hangar, but found no other exit. Again he pulled frantically at the weighty panels, but they would not give a fraction of an inch.

A stifling silence closed around Tim Donovan as he realized he was a helpless prisoner....

IN AN operations-office in the headquarters of the Second Corps Area, on Governors Island, in New York Bay, Z-7 peered at terse reports which had come to him by radio. His fingers drummed the desk anxiously until a quick step sounded in the corridor. He rose expectantly, his black eyes smouldering, as Operator 5 opened the door.

Jimmy Christopher's left arm was suspended in a sling. It had suffered a ragged cut during his plunge to earth in the broken gyro. A line of bandage marked his high forehead. His face was drawn and his eyes were anxious, yet his step was brisk and his grip firm when he took Z-7's hand.

"I've just landed, Chief, thanks to your providing me with a plane. I started back as soon as I finished examining the field."

"I'm glad you escaped with no worse injuries," the Washington chief answered. "Have you anything to add to these reports?"

Operator 5 took the proffered flimsies. As he glanced at them, he asked anxiously: "Chief, has there been any word from Tim Donovan?"

"Nothing."

"You haven't located the army plane I saw on the field last night?"

"No."

"And the information I requested?"

"It is being checked on now. I'm expecting a report by telephone at any—"

The desk instrument rang even as Z-7 spoke. He listened over the wire while Operator 5 read the reports he had sent by short wave wireless from the secret field in Pennsylvania. His call to Headquarters MW had brought Intelligence men to the spot by dawn. Z-7 had ordered a plane for Operator 5, and he had used its transmitter to flash his information to New York during his return flight.

... MW-NY... SECRET FIELD DESTROYED BY PLANTED MINES... PROJECTING DEVICE TOTALLY WRECKED... NO CLUES AS TO ITS USE... OR AS TO IDENTITY OF LEADER OF SECRET LOYALISTS... ALL MEMBERS OF BAND ESCAPED... OPERATOR 5.

As Z-7 replaced the telephone, Jimmy Christopher observed grimly: "There is nothing to add, Chief. The Loyalists destroyed their projector rather than to disclose their secret."

Z-7 had made notes during his conversation on the wire. He referred to them as he observed: "Washington has supplied the information you asked for. It was found in certain secret files that were begun when the nation was created. They have scarcely been touched in the past hundred years. It refers to espionage work for the Crown, conducted during the American Revolution, under the direction of a British officer, Major Lloyd Brennock."

"Yes, Chief?" Operator 5 leaned forward.

"The report is brief. Though espionage is as old as history

itself, the British made no particular steps toward organizing an intelligence until Cromwell. It is not generally known, but their information office was functioning at the time the American colonies declared their independence. In the war that followed, espionage work against the colonists was handled by the officer then in charge of the British information office—the Major Brennock whose name you heard mentioned last night so reverently by the leader of the Secret Loyalists.

"The Loyalists, at the time of the Revolution," Z-7 explained, "were those who opposed our independence. The weight of their influence, by means of propaganda, was thrown against the fighting colonists by the secret activities of Major Brennock. This report describes him as an almost insanely ambitious man who considered his work more important to the British cause than armed battle. His service to George III was downright worship. This information closes with a hint that Brennock continued his secret operations even after the signing of the Treaty of Yorktown in September, 1783."

Z-7'S SMOLDERING eyes searched Jimmy Christopher's. "Major Brennock has been dead much longer than a century. The Secret Loyalists we are investigating now can have no connection with the espionage service he operated for the Crown during the American Revolution."

Operator 5's lips pursed. "Whatever the Secret Loyalists were when the colonies claimed their independence—whatever they were yesterday, when the first attack struck—they have taken on an entirely different character today."

"What do you mean by that?"

Jimmy Christopher smiled. "You know my methods, Chief. I never formulate theories until I am sure of facts. When our investigation has made more progress—" He broke off, his manner quickening as he glanced at the electric desk clock. "There's no time to waste if we're to make our tests. Are the preparations finished?"

"The ray finders and the stratospheric balloon are ready. Come with me."

As Operator 5 opened the door for Z-7, his eyes widened with surprise. A girl, hurrying along the corridor, greeted him with a warm smile. She gave the Washington chief only a brief glance in her eagerness to reach Jimmy Christopher. She seized his hand anxiously as she asked:

"Jimmy, what have you been doing? What are you up to now? You've been working on this case night and day for weeks, and Dad and I have scarcely seen you. You aren't keeping secrets from me, are you, Jimmy?"

"Not from you, Di," he answered with a quiet laugh. "I couldn't if I tried. There's scarcely any time to explain now, but you'll understand everything in a moment."

"Good!" she exclaimed. "I made MW tell me you were expected here, and I came right away. You know you can count on me for all the help I can give you, Jimmy."

"I'm sure of it, Di."

Diane Elliot hurried along the corridor with Operator 5. Her resourcefulness and self-reliance had earned her an enviable position as special correspondent for the far-flung Amalgamated Press. Her avid search for sensational news had led her to her first meeting with Jimmy Christopher during his work on a dangerous espionage case in San Francisco. Since then she had aided him greatly in carrying out important special orders. Operator 5 had learned he could rely on her in the most trying emergency.

She hastened at his side, after Z-7, down a long flight of cement stairs. The Washington chief opened an iron door to reveal a second flight. He explained, as they went down with him, that they were about to enter a room which many of the officers of the Second Corps Area Headquarters did not know existed. It had been provided as an emergency retreat in case of armed attack, and was not shown on any plan. When they paused at another metal door, they were far below the surface of the bay.

At Z-7's knock, a bolt creaked and the entrance opened. They stepped toward a table bearing a strange apparatus. Long quartz tubes were suspended on standards. Two men in smocks—physicists from a federal laboratory in Washington—were painstakingly checking the wires which led to banks of storage batteries. They scarcely glanced up as Operator 5 looked at the walls.

Gray sheets of lead had been applied over every square inch. The floor and the ceiling were also layered with it. The metal covered even the single door. It gave the underground room the aspect of an impregnable vault, yet Operator 5's voice was edged with anxiety as he asked: "Are you sure, gentlemen, that the plates are thick enough to ward off the ray?"

THE SCIENTISTS smiled slowly. "Four inches of sheeting have been applied. It would shield us from any force similar to

X-rays or radioactive emanations. The only force known to our experience that can penetrate to us here are the Cosmic Rays, which, of course, do not destroy life."*

"You are ready to analyze the beam, in case it reaches this point?"

"Yes. These are Geiger counter tubes. They are the most sensitive apparatus in the world for the purpose.** Coupled as they

---

* AUTHOR'S NOTE: Scientists discovered only recently the mysterious emanations which are constantly bombarding the earth from the farthest reaches of interstellar space. These rays do not come from any one point, but from all points at once. Conflicting theories have been advanced to explain the Cosmic Rays. Gravitation pulls them toward the earth with a force of billions of volts, but it is not certainly known whether they result from the creation of matter in space or its destruction. These particular impulses, of course, are harmless to life.

** AUTHOR'S NOTE: Geiger counter tubes were used recently in a Cosmic Ray experiment in New York City. Two of these devices were placed in a bank vault located under the Ruppert Building, at Broadway and 44th Street. They were forty feet underground and imprisoned by 360 tons of concrete and chromium steel. Above them the building reared 34 stories, 430 feet.

The tubes were mounted end to end and pointed straight up. The only ray which could possibly penetrate them must come from directly above, penetrating the entire height of the building and the top of the vault. Thick lead was placed beneath them to shield them from any radiation which might come up from the earth. It was a dramatic and historic moment when the switch was closed. The loud-speaker merely gave forth a series of clicks, as the tubes registered the reception of a ray, but it meant that the Cosmic Rays are to photographic spectroscopes, we hope we can analyze any impulses that reach us."

Operator 5's eyes grew solemn. "Gentlemen, there is a reason why you were not ordered, but asked to volunteer, for this task. The death beam is the most powerful destructive agency in existence. It may be able to pierce the earth, and these thicknesses of lead, as though nothing were in the way. If they do, you understand, you will suffer instantaneous, paralytic death."

Again the two scientists smiled. "We are aware of the danger."

Operator 5 extended his hand. The two men gripped it silently, and turned back to their work. With no thought of self, but absorbed in a scientific mystery, they remained inside the lead-walled room as Z-7, Operator 5 and Diane Elliot went out the door and securely closed it.

They did not speak while they climbed the two long flights. Z-7 led the way from the operations-building to Jay Field. It had been cleared of all service craft except the monoplane which had carried Operator 5 from the Pennsylvania wilderness. At its center, the half-filled ball of a huge balloon was tugging at the ropes which held it captive. Beneath it dangled the spherical gondola designed for a voyage into the highest stratum of the world's atmospheric envelope.

Tank after tank of helium had been released into the bag, and

possessed tremendous penetrating power. It was further found that they issued from every point in the sky at which the tubes were pointed. Whatever their origin, it is certain they are the product of cataclysmic events of such enormous power that the human mind cannot grasp the elements involved.

they now lay empty in a neat stack. Allowance had been made for the swelling of the gas in the regions of low air-pressure miles above the earth. A control cord was connected from a release valve to a special mechanism operated from within the metal sphere. The outer surface of the gondola was painted black so that the absorbed heat of the sun might warm the occupants during the flight in the upper zones where temperatures of eighty degrees below zero had been recorded. Through the open port, Operator 5 saw that all except the most essential instruments had been removed to facilitate the ascent.

An officer in fur-lined flying suit stepped alertly toward Z-7.

"Ready, sir," he reported. "We must take off at once if we hope to reach the stratosphere by high noon."

"This young man," Z-7 answered with an approving nod, "is your passenger."

Lieutenant Parsons smiled. "The purpose of the ascent has been explained to me," he observed, "but I must warn you that it entails considerable danger. I have already made one flight into the stratosphere, and I speak from experience.

"This bag is perfectly sound, now, but it may fail without the lightest notice. Any microscopic defect may become a rip that will release all the gas almost instantly. If that happens, it means an unrestricted drop of miles to the earth—certain destruction."

OPERATOR 5'S smile answered the stratospheric pilot. "I know. It is also true that once we're up, we're at the mercy of the winds and may be carried far out to sea. It may be that we will float directly into the path of the death beam, and that will transform us into stiffened corpses floating between the worlds. You are running the same chances as I. Can we take off at once?"

"All set."

"Jimmy!" Diane Elliot's hand closed on Operator 5's arm. "Don't say no, and don't argue, because it won't do a bit of good—because I'm going with you."

Jimmy Christopher blurted: "It's impossible, Di! You've just heard what we're facing. I can't let you risk that."

"You simply can't stop me, Jimmy," the girl countered. "If something happens to you up there, I want it to happen to me, too. If nothing comes of it, there's no harm done. Even if we don't learn anything about the death beam, it will make a gorgeous story for the Amalgamated. There! I'm going!"

Before Operator 5 could stop her, Diane ran to the short ladder. She was halfway in the metal shell when he seized her arm. She laughingly resisted, and succeeded in slipping through. He gazed at her eager eyes in dismay, for he knew no persuasion could bring her out now. He looked around to see Lieutenant Parsons' head wagging. He observed with grim warnings:

"It's no use, Lieutenant."

"Her weight may be enough to keep us out of the highest air," Parsons observed gravely. "And it may cause a defect to open in the bag which would otherwise hold. In any case, we've got to take off at once."

"Signal readiness."

At Parsons' gesture, the ground-crew sprang into action. Operator 5 paused at the gondola ladder as Z-7 came to him solemnly. Their hands gripped as the Washington chief asked:

"You think the beam will strike again, even though the projector on the secret field in Pennsylvania was destroyed?"

"I feel sure of it, Chief. The Secret Loyalists have planned long and carefully. They have not built their whole strategy on a single machine. There must be others ready for use. I hope this flight will help solve the mystery of the beam."

"Good luck, my boy!"

"Thanks, Chief."

Jimmy Christopher climbed quickly through the port. Diane Elliot smiled as he came to her side, but now there was a flicker of uncertainty in her eyes. She lifted her chin confidently as Lieutenant Parsons crawled into the metal ball. They spoke no word while the chief of the ground-crew quickly closed the port and tightened the stout bolts.

The sphere became hermetically sealed. Immediately Parsons released the valve of a tank strapped to the curving wall. A low, hissing sound indicated a flow of gas into the enclosed space. Operator 5 checked the operation of the dioxide absorbent and found it functioning perfectly. Upon these two devices they must depend for air to breathe during the hours in the air. Parsons, gazing out the port, signaled again, and the gondola bobbed.

Z-7 watched the operation of releasing the huge balloon intently. One by one, the shrouds were freed until only three lines pinioned the swaying bag. The officer in command of the Governors Island Headquarters came briskly to his side while preparations were in progress.

"You understand. Colonel," the Washington chief said gravely, "that every man must be ordered from the island? When high

JOBERT

noon strikes, there must be absolutely no one in this headquarters except the two scientists in the underground room. You have given your instructions?"

"I have. At noon the island will be deserted."

From the chief of the ground crew a sharp command rang: "Cut loose!"

BRENNOCK

Sharp knives severed the three remaining shrouds of the balloon at the same instant. Instantly the bag and the gondola sprang upward. It rose with amazing speed while the ground crew and the officers watched with caught breath. It drifted slightly on the wind as it sailed above the island. Higher and higher it soared toward the roof of the earth. It became a mere

63

dot floating in the blue. At last it dissolved away in the emptiness of space....

CHAPTER 4
STORM BETWEEN WORLDS

Z-7 STRODE anxiously into his office in the lofty suite which comprised secret Intelligence Headquarters MW. He glanced quickly at reports waiting for him on his desk, and quickly singled one out. The black of his eyes flashed as he read:

...FIRST REPORT... ASCENT SMOOTH... HEIGHT NOW FIVE MILES... ALL WELL... OPERATOR 5....

Z-7 glanced at the electric clock. The stratospheric bag, he knew, must at least double its elevation during the few minutes remaining until high noon. He strode through a door, into the wireless communications-room. As he passed one of the black panels, the attendant passed him a fresh flimsy. He quickly read the message:

...REPORT TWO... CLIMBING RAPIDLY... ELEVATION EIGHT MILES... INSTRUMENTS FUNCTIONING PERFECTLY... VISIBILITY EXCELLENT... OPERATOR 5....

The words had flashed from the wireless equipment carried in the gondola now soaring far above the earth's surface. The impulses received in MW were the only bond connecting the passengers of the balloon with the world below. Z-7's eyes gleamed with satisfaction as he instructed the wireless operator:

"Signal Operator 5 his reports are being received clearly. Keep on his wave constantly."

The Washington chief took a pair of powerful binoculars to the window near the panel. New York lay like a crustacean growth below him. In the spreading blue of the bay, Governors Island was clearly visible. Z-7 focused his lenses on it and studied every visible inch.

He had remained at the Second Corps Area headquarters until every officer had left by plane and boat. Having made sure that the buildings and fields were deserted, he had come directly to Manhattan. No one remained on the island now, except the two government scientists in the room far underground.

Z-7 turned as a door opened, and the communications-chief brought him a teletype report. It was coded Washington and bore the signature of the Chief of Staff.

... MW-NY... SPECIAL ATTENTION Z-7... BRIGA-DIER GENERAL BRAXTON REPORTED MISSING... LAST SEEN LEAVING NEW YORK BY PLANE DESTI-NATION WASHINGTON... NO WORD SINCE TAKE-OFF... HAS NOT ARRIVED BOLLING OR AT ANY FIELD ALONG AIR ROUTE... PLANE ALSO MISS-ING... LANE SEARCHED IN VAIN... URGE INVES-TIGATION OF POSSIBLE CONNECTION BETWEEN BRAXTON'S DISAPPEARANCE AND ATTACKS OF DEATH BEAM... FALK....

Z-7 peered baffled at the message. The attendant at the wireless receiver thrust another report at him. New information had flashed out of the zenith:

REPORT THREE... STILL RISING SWIFTLY... CONDITIONS PERFECT... DRIFTING SLIGHTLY INLAND BUT HOLDING POSITION EXCELLENTLY... GOVERNORS ISLAND VISIBLE IN TELESCOPE... ELEVATION ABOVE TEN MILES... OPERATOR 5....

THE WASHINGTON chief watched the spinning second-hand of the electric clock. His burning impatience increased with each minute that brought noon closer, he held his binoculars ready at the window as the attendant at the second wireless board looked up wonderingly.

"I am picking up very weak signals, Chief. They are so faint I can't piece them together. This is the fourth time I've caught them since dawn. I've no idea where they're coming from, but they might mean something."

Z-7 urged: "Keep trying to bring them up."

At the third panel, another attendant looked up. "That's strange," he observed. "I'm getting some unusual signals too, but they can't be the same. They're very distinct, but they mean nothing. They're a series of spaced dots, and each time they sound I hear the radio echo. It's as though someone were using special instruments to sound the elevation of the Kennelly-Heaviside layer."

The Washington chief asked alertly: "Have you ever heard them before?"

"Yes, sir. I picked them up shortly before the Air Corps display yesterday. If they have any connection—"

"Great Scott!" Z-7 blurted. "Signal our naval direction finders to try to locate the source of those impulses. It may be connected in some way with—"

"No use, chief," the third attendant broke in and he listened intently through his phones. "They're gone again."

A new dread came to Z-7's heart as his mind mulled over the information. Again he turned his binoculars on Governors Island. In the teeming Bay, it lay as deserted as though it were lost in some remote sea. He turned quickly as an exclamation came from the attendant who was awaiting further reports from the soaring gondola. Eagerly he read the scrawl:

... REPORT FOUR... SPEED OF ASCENT HAS SHARPLY DECREASED... HAVE REACHED HEIGHT EQUALING ANY PREVIOUS STRATOSPHERIC FLIGHT... ELEVATION APPROACHING THIRTEEN MILES... DRIFTING SLIGHTLY... HOLD READY FOR OBSERVATIONS AT NOON... OPERATOR 5....

Z-7 knew that the chronometer of the super-stratum gondola had been adjusted and checked with utmost care. It was registering Naval Observatory time with an accuracy tested within a fraction of a second. The clocks in MW had been synchronized with it. Z-7's nerves tightened with grim expectancy.

Sixty seconds would bring high noon.

Silence held over Governors Island. The offices, the barracks, the shops were empty. Jay Field was as desolate as a desert, with only the plane of Operator 5 remaining in the open. Stakes and piled tanks marked the spot from which the stratospheric craft had left the surface of the earth. The pall of quiet continued as the last minute before noon ticked away. In the underground room, the two government scientists gazed alertly at a clock which was also synchronized with that carried in the gondola. Their Geiger counter tubes were ready. Every connection had been checked and rechecked. Their meters were registering a steady flow of current which activated the supersensitive ray receivers. A loudspeaker was ready to reproduce the clicking noises which must result if any radiating energy plunged through the quartz tubes. They waited tensely while the seconds passed....

MILES UP in the sky the stratospheric balloon floated. The earth presented a weird appearance through the ports of the metal shell. It was now a brilliant, reddish color, surrounded by an aura of beautiful blue. It had lost the semblance of a sphere and seemed to be a disc with up-curved edge. Few details of its surface were discernible to the naked eye between the patches of clouds floating over it. Yet Operator 5, peering downward through a sealed port, was able to distinguish the outline of Governors Island.

Diane Elliot watched Jimmy Christopher anxiously while Lieutenant Parsons checked the sensitive instruments. The air inside the frail shell was being constantly replenished, while that outside was far too rarefied to support human life. The temperature within the gondola was comfortably warm, due to the absorption of the sun's radiations on the black surface, though the thermocouple indicated eighty-five degrees below zero in the surrounding element. The bag above the metal sphere had fattened to its full extent. Its pressure was kept under close check by Lieutenant Parsons while the craft floated across the roof of the world.

Fifteen seconds until noon....

Jimmy Christopher turned quickly to the wireless equipment. He tapped a message which flashed through thirteen miles of ether to the receivers in MW:

... REPORT FIVE... POSITION SLIGHTLY WEST OF GOVERNORS ISLAND... OBSERVATIONS BEING MADE... IF SHAFT APPEARS IT MUST PASS TO EAST OF US... A STORM NOW BREWING IN THE STRATOSPHERE BUT OTHERWISE NO UNUSUAL INDICATIONS... OPERATOR 5....

The gondola had begun to toss in the rarefied air. Jimmy Christopher noted concern in Parsons' eyes as he turned to the port looking eastward. He knew that the upper reaches of the atmosphere were usually flowing in a steady prevailing wind. Previous observations had not reported any storms in the tranquil regions bordering on the empty space between the worlds. Yet now a tempest was tearing the thin air above and beyond the balloon with increasing violence.

It had come without warning out of the nothingness of the stratosphere. The growing roar of the tempest filled the gondola with a deafening thunder. Operator 5 pressed the phones of the wireless receiver close to his ears, in preparation for reporting the phenomenon, but to his dismay he heard the ear-splitting rumble reproduced in the diaphragms. He found communication impossible. The balloon tossed wildly as he flung himself to the Eastward port and peered up.

"It's happening far above us!" he shouted through the turmoil. "Release the pressure on the bag or it will burst!"

Lieutenant Parsons frantically pulled the valve lever. Diane Elliot braced herself while Operator 5 strove to keep his position. The rolling and lurching of the craft spilled them about. The turmoil in the thin, outer air exceeded any violent storm in Jimmy Christopher's experience. He clung to the handholds desperately and continued to peer into the lofty region where cataclysmic forces were battling.

Lieutenant Parsons cried through the uproar: "High noon! High noon!"

AT THAT instant, the brilliant violet beam appeared! The colored shaft streaked straight downward past the tossing shell. It seemed to taper to a point, like a sword, as it struck to the surface of the earth. Its direction was exactly vertical. During the second of its existence, Operator 5's widened eyes followed it upward. He saw it originating in the region of storm. It was springing out of empty space!

The savage turmoil of the stratosphere was whirling the balloon closer to the purplish beam. The brilliance of the color became almost blinding as Operator 5 watched it streaming closer. He knew that once the gondola swung inside the shaft, instantaneous death would strike through the shell. "We will become corpses floating between the worlds" he had said on Jay Field—and now that horrible doom threatened! The movement of the craft was dazzlingly swift as the raging cosmic forces sucked it toward the violet column of death.

The purple color was beginning to shine inside the shell when, as suddenly as it had appeared, the shaft vanished. It passed out of existence with the swiftness of lightning. Its whole length disappeared at the same instant. Operator 5 fell back, groping for the wireless key, as the balloon continued to toss. The violent storm had subsided during the beam's existence, but now it struck again as powerfully as before.

Jimmy Christopher clung desperately as he flashed his message:

BEAM HAS STRUCK… INVESTIGATE RESULTS!

He whirled to the bewildered Parsons and snapped an imperative command:

"Down! Go down!"

The officer pulled frantically on the release valve. The raging of the storm continued as helium escaped swiftly from the bag. The gondola descended with increasing speed. Operator 5 threw himself again to the port, and peered into the lofty regions where the tempest was raging. Long moments passed while the shell drifted downward. At last the cosmic fury subsided.

Tranquility returned to the atmosphere as Jimmy Christopher directed a pair of powerful binoculars through the port. He swept the entire region of faint blue with the lenses. When he drew back, eyes narrowed and puzzled, he was certain no other craft was hovering in the stratosphere....

A SPEED boat cut a white wake across New York Bay. Stinging spray flew over those who clung to its rail. Operator 5, with Diane Elliot at his side, peered across the swells at the looming expanse of Governors Island. Z-7's black eyes smoldered ominously as he blurted into the wind:

"I've been unable to raise the underground room by telephone. It's possible the beam put the line out of commission. God, I hope those men have discovered the nature of the beam!"

Under Jimmy Christopher's orders, the stratospheric balloon had descended as rapidly as possible. Pulled in one direction, then another, by the prevailing winds of the successive strata of the air, they had maneuvered to earth as close as possible to the point of their ascent. Constant wireless messengers had kept Z-7 posted on their progress. By the time they had come down near the Palisades, the Washington chief had had a boat waiting. While Lieutenant Parsons remained with the deflated balloon, the craft had started down the river at top speed.

"You saw the beam strike, Chief?" Jimmy Christopher asked.

"I did! It came like a bolt of purple lightning, without a sound. It covered all of Governors Island with a purple glow. The instant it disappeared, I tried to reach the underground room by phone. When that failed, I asked the commanding officer to go across. He's there now, with his men."

The boat swerved toward a pier. Operator 5 hastily made it fast, helped Diane up, then hurried at Z-7's side to the operations-office. Voices rumbled in the depths of the stairwell as they descended the stone flights. A sharp hissing sound grew louder when they neared the bottom. The brilliant flame of an acetylene torch was cutting into the metal of the lower door, directed by an officer wearing black goggles. The commander turned smartly as Z-7, Operator 5 and the girl came to a stop.

"We haven't been able to make them hear, sir. The bolt is still in place. The only way we can get in is to cut the door away."

"Go ahead with it!"

Operator 5 waited tensely, his heart filled with dread, while he watched the sibilant flame cut through the metal with the ease of a knife slicing butter. Molten drops fell sparkling as the tongue traced a square. The man stepped back as the section sagged and fell with a clang. Jimmy Christopher was the first to duck through the opening. Just inside, with Z-7 crowding behind him, he came to a startled stop.

The two government scientists were standing at the table. The hand of one was poised on the black knob of a control unit. The other was bent forward in the act of making a notation on a pad, but his pencil scarcely touched the paper. The meters were still registering the activity of the Geiger counter tubes. Uncannily, the two men kept their positions without the slightest movement.

Operator 5 whispered: "Dead."

Z-7 took slow steps forward. He stared appalled at the fixed expressions on the faces of the two scientists. They evinced intense interest, but not the slightest pain or surprise. It was as though an evil magic wand had transformed them into statues.

"The beam struck here with full force," the Washington chief

73

The scientists were standing at the table, petrified as statues!

exclaimed. "Through the earth and the metal sheeting! They died before they could make their tests!"

Operator 5 observed grimly: "Nothing can stop that power, Chief—nothing!"

Z-7's black eyes blazed. "You saw no craft in the sky that could have shot out the beam? You learned absolutely nothing about the nature or the source of the force? Do you mean our attempt has completely failed?"

"We learned one valuable fact, Z-7," Operator 5 answered

quietly. "There is no machine which directly generates the death power. It is wielded by man, but it is not man-made. The truth is that it originates in interstellar space. It's so potent it's capable of destroying every living thing on the face of the earth. Of that, Chief, we can now be absolutely certain!"

CHAPTER 5
CAPTIVE'S SIGNAL

POSSESSED BY a torturous agitation, Z-7 paced his office in MW. He had returned alone from Governors Island shortly after the discovery of the corpses in the underground room. Later, a report by telephone had informed him of Operator 5's return to Manhattan. Having taken Diane Elliot to the home of his father, Jimmy Christopher had come to MW. He had inquired anxiously concerning Tim Donovan. Told there was no news, he had hurried into the scientific laboratory. He was still working behind its locked doors as Z-7 strode back and forth anxiously. Hours had passed, and dusk was descending over the city.

The communications chief brought a report, hot off the teletype wires, to Z-7's desk:

... MW-NY... BRIGADIER GENERAL BRAXTON STILL MISSING... ABSOLUTELY NO TRACE OF HIM... OR PLANE... BROTHER, CAPTAIN BRAXTON, INSISTS HE HAD PLANNED TO RETURN DIRECTLY TO HIS OFFICE BUT HE NEVER

REACHED BOLLING… INSIST THIS MATTER BE INVESTIGATED BY OPERATOR 5… FALK….

Z-7's eyes narrowed thoughtfully. He looked up when one of the agents assigned to wireless duty came quickly into the room.

"Chief, you instructed me this noon to try to decipher the weak signals that have been sounding all day. They are still coming in, but I can't make head nor tail of them. Now that it's getting dark, they may grow stronger. Shall I keep on the job?"

"By all means!"

Z-7's fingers drummed. He realized that, except for Operator 5's warning, every man on Governors Island would have been struck by the paralytic death. Like Mitchell Field, it would have become a post of the doomed. Z-7 had the reports of the necropsies performed on the bodies of the two scientists, but the information was completely negative. The violet beam remained a baffling puzzle, promising horrible eventualities.

The Washington chief looked up as the door opened quickly and Jimmy Christopher strode into the office. Operator 5's eyes shone with grim elation as he drew a chair close and fingered the voluminous notes he had taken. Softly he reported:

"I believe I have the answer, Chief."

"In God's name, what is it?"

Jimmy Christopher made each word clear as he explained. "The earth is flying through space which is filled with terrific forces. They are the powers which helped create the universe, which even now are working to build it higher or destroy it. Theories about these forces are imperfect and conflicting, because the study is so new that only a few scientists know the full details. As an example, there is the research being made into the nature of the Cosmic Rays by Dr. R. A. Millikan, one of the world's greatest physicists."

"I have read of Dr. Millikan's experiments, and of the conclusion of Sir James Jeans about the Cosmic Rays," Z-7 commented.

"We are only now gathering data on these mysterious forces that play through interstellar space," Operator 5 continued. "What I am about to tell you now is the discovery of Dr. Charles G. Abbott, secretary of the Smithsonian Institution, and his secretary, I. B. Aldrich, made at the Mount Wilson observatory in California recently. It concerns the existence of huge 'stars of death'." *

Z-7 LISTENED intently as Operator 5 continued:

"These men, with a new set-up of instruments, made the most delicate measurements ever achieved of the energy of various wave-lengths or colors of radiations coming from different kinds of stars. They measured almost infinitesimal amounts of star radiation that reach the earth after traveling for years across trillions and quadrillions of miles. They discovered stars which are literally too hot to be bright."

Unless one minutely studies the fascinating mysteries of cosmic space, Operator 5 explained further, the facts seem incredible on first hearing, yet there is no doubt of their truth.

---

* AUTHOR'S NOTE: The discovery of the existence of "death stars" was announced in an Associated Press dispatch dated October 2, 1934, by the Smithsonian Institution.

One unnamed, far-off star has a temperature of 180,000 degrees Fahrenheit—the highest heat ever measured anywhere, according to a report of a conference on spectroscopy held recently at the Massachusetts Institute of Technology. The surface of our sun, by comparison, is a mere 10,000 degrees, while on the earth's surface water boils at a temperature of only 212 degrees Fahrenheit. This, Operator 5 pointed out, was one of the wonders of cosmology which the human mind is almost incapable of grasping.

"Other stars," Jimmy Christopher went on, "have a surface temperature of 36,000 degrees. Among these, virtually all of the blue-colored stars are of the death type. This means that certain stars are emitting a vast shower of death rays which are known to be ultra-violet radiations of very short wave-lengths. There are many of these huge stars. A typical star of death is Rigel, in the left foot of the constellation of Orion."

"You mean these stars are literally spraying a murderous force throughout all space?" Z-7 asked in astonishment.

"Exactly that, Chief. The earth and all other planets of the solar system are being constantly bombarded."

"But this power doesn't reach the surface of the earth. What protects us from it?"

"A layer of ozone, high in the atmosphere, screens it out.*

---

* AUTHOR'S NOTE: Ozone is the element oxygen in an unusual molecular form. While the chemical symbol for oxygen is O, that for ozone is O_3. It is formed by the slow oxidation of many substances. Country air contains one volume of ozone to 700,000 volumes of air.

Without that protective skin of gas, no life would be possible on this planet. If it breaks, and the death rays stream through—you have seen the result."

Z-7 sprang to his feet "That's the answer?"

"Precisely." Operator 5's words rushed. The storm I witnessed in the stratosphere was actually the puncturing of the stratum of ozone. A projector, like the one I found on the secret field in Pennsylvania, must have caused it. An ionized beam, striking into the ozone, caused it to change its molecular structure and break down into oxygen. Ozone is a denser gas than oxygen, and the change in volume caused the storm. Literally, the way was opened for the rays of the death stars to plunge through to the earth!"

"Whoever devised that devilish contrivance," Z-7 declared slowly, "is able to aim it with crafty exactness."

"Yes. The height of the layer of ozone is constantly changing, like the Kennelly-Heaviside ceiling,* but the distance can be found at any time through the use of radio echoes. Once the

---

* AUTHOR'S NOTE: The sun bombards the earth with streams of electrons like a gigantic cathode ray tube. Striking our outer atmosphere, they break up into positive and negative ions. This blanket of electrific particles, called the Kennelly-Heaviside layer, hovers at variable distances above the earth's surface, depending on atmospheric conditions and the extent of sun-spots. Its average height is about seventy miles. It serves as a gigantic mirror, reflecting sky-bound radio waves back to earth. It is only because of this reflection that wireless impulses are able to travel long distances, even around the globe.

height is known, it is possible, of course, to train the projector on it at an exact spot. The rays of the death stars, streaming out of cosmic space, strike through in a perfectly vertical shaft. They can be directed at any point as accurately as artillery fire."

"Then space itself is generating the power that is attacking us, and the machines of the Secret Loyalists merely release it?" Z-7 queried. "How the devil can we protect ourselves from that power?"

"There is absolutely no way of shielding ourselves from it after it has broken through the ozone layer," Operator 5 answered gravely. "We can only hope to destroy the projectors that liberate it."

Z-7 gestured his despair. "Destroy them? Where are they? We're helpless until—"

"We haven't the slightest clue to the location of the machines, Chief—but our very existence depends upon our finding them." A SHARP knock sounded on the office door as it opened. The wireless operator looked in and spoke quickly:

"The signals are stronger now, Z-7. I've been able to catch a few words. I'm not sure, but I think the message is being sent to Operator 5."

"I'll listen in!"

Jimmy Christopher strode into the wireless communications-room. As the Operator 5 sat at the panel, he pressed phones to his ears and listened intently. A faint dot-dash sputter tightened his nerves. He recognized the manner of the sender as easily as he might a familiar voice, though he could distinguish no word.

"Tim!" he exclaimed. "Tim's sending this code!"

"He's been trying to reach us all day," Z-7 explained quickly. "Catch that message if you possibly can. It may mean a new lead to the commander of the Secret Loyalists."

Operator 5 strove to piece the fragmentary letters together as he answered: "Flash the naval radio direction finders to chart the impulses, Chief. That will tell us where Tim is, even if the message doesn't come through."

Z-7's crackling orders sent another of the wireless experts into action while Operator 5 continued to listen. The few letters caught by Jimmy Christopher's keen ears were meaningless. The sputtering stopped, then began again. Operator 5 directed quickly:

"Signal the Intelligence cars to be held ready, Chief. Put a dozen men in them. I have a hunch Tim isn't far away. He must have kept with the plane until it reached its destination and now—"

Jimmy Christopher's voice trailed off as the Washington chief snapped orders into a telephone. The wireless attendants kept alert at their boards. Crackling signals answered in the phones of the men who had flashed the naval direction finders. He swung away to refer to a chart, then intently consulted a detailed photographic map of New York City and environs which covered one wall of the room. Operator 5 straightened suddenly.

"A little of it's coming through! 'Held—prisoner—hangar.' It's fading again." A tense minute passed. "Now it's coming back. 'Using transmitter of army plane—hidden here. Cannot give location—' It's gone!"

"I have it!"

Operator 5 spun to the man at the map. He had swung long, narrow pointers across it in accordance with the reports radioed from the direction-finder stations. They crossed at a point north of the city. The area was one occupied by spacious estates in Westchester. Jimmy Christopher noted exultantly that the point of convergence lay directly upon the roof of a low building in the photograph.

"Tim's calling from there! Come on, Chief!"

He hurried from the communications-room, heart speeding with the hope that Tim's message might bring him again on the trail of the merciless leader of the Secret Loyalists.

THREE INTELLIGENCE machines paraded swiftly over the road leading to the estate which the tracers had indicated on the map in Headquarters MW. Operator 5 tensed at the wheel of the Diesel-engined roadster leading the way. Its tires whined as he followed sharp bends. His foot shot to the brakes when a massive stone gateway appeared. The beams of the headlamps shafted through it as he stepped out.

"Plane taking off!" Z-7 exclaimed.

The droning exhaust was pulsing loudly through the night. Operator 5 peered past a lightless mansion, across dark grounds. He saw no wing beacons to indicate the presence of the craft, but in a moment, a pouring stream of fire appeared. It was flowing from the exhaust stacks of a moving crate. The plane thundered across the ground, gathering speed, as Jimmy Christopher slipped back into the car.

"Calling MW!" He sang the words into the microphone of

the two-way radio equipment of the roadster while the roar of the plane continued. "Calling MW!"

"MW answering."

"Special orders! Flash Jay Field that a plane is taking off from a point north of Manhattan. It is to be trailed if possible. Order the best pilot on the island to trace it. I'll give you its direction in a moment."

"Standing by!"

Operator 5 gazed into the star-sprinkled sky. Black wings were swooping across it. Still without lights, the plane was driving into a sharp climb. Jimmy Christopher's eyes followed it while it banked toward the Hudson. Immediately it leveled and deadheaded. Again he spoke sharply into the microphone:

"MW! The plane is coursing due south. It is an army pursuit. If possible, it is to be forced down and its pilot made prisoner. Fastest handling on those orders.

"I have Jay Field on the wire now."

Jimmy Christopher stepped from the car to find Z-7 impatiently pressing a bell button at the gate. The call was bringing no response. The grounds were a black void. Every window of the mansion was lightless. The Intelligence men gathered around Z-7 and bore their weight against the gate, but its massive lock held. Z-7 abandoned the button with an angry exclamation.

Grimly Operator 5 promised: "We're going in, Chief."

He returned to the wheel of his roadster. Skillfully he brought the front bumper in contact with the bars of the gate. When he released the clutch, the rear tires spun in the grit, but the motor exerted a powerful force. Jimmy Christopher persisted until an ear-stinging snap sounded. The broken bolt of the lock opened the way. The roadster jounced through and the Intelligence men sprang after it.

Operator 5 sent the car whirling past the rear of the mansion. The beams of the headlights swung like glittering blades across the spreading lawn. Jimmy Christopher sprang from the wheel and urgently called: "Tim! Old Timer! Where are you?" He brought his automatic into his hand, peering around. An exclamation of satisfaction passed his lips as a flicker of movement showed in the glare and a call answered:

"Jimmy! Here!"

TIM DONOVAN came running from the direction of the disguised hangar. Its doors yawned open behind him. He stumbled to a breathless stop, grinning with delight In his eagerness he flung his arms around Operator 5.

"Gee, Jimmy! I thought my message wasn't being picked up! I've been locked in the hangar twenty hours, trying to get you on the transmitter of the army plane. Gosh, I'm glad to see you!"

"You're worn out, old timer." Jimmy Christopher saw that Tim was suffering from hunger and thirst. "We could scarcely catch your signals, probably because the walls of the hangar are metal and grounded. Who took the plane up a minute ago? Did you see him, Tim?"

"Not his face, Jimmy," the boy answered breathlessly. "He was masked. It was the same man who brought the plane here last night. I'm sure it isn't Apito, because I heard him called by name. It was Jobert."

"Jobert!" Operator 5 echoed in dismay. "Arnes Jobert is one

of the most dangerous men in the world. He is a destructive radical and a revolutionist. Somehow he smuggled himself into the United States a year ago and began to build up a powerful subversive organization. Jobert—the new leader of the Secret Loyalists!"

"What's that?" The voice came out of the darkness. Z-7, hurrying close, had heard the name. "What the devil does it mean, Operator 5? Jobert pays no allegiance to any nation, let alone the Empire of Great Britain. Why should he be leading an espionage system which originated in Revolutionary times?"

"He has usurped the leadership of the Secret Loyalists, Chief—it can mean nothing else," Operator 5 explained quickly. "For a hundred and fifty years, it has been a secret society like those in Europe.* Last night it became transformed—"

* AUTHOR'S NOTE: The secret societies of Europe have sometimes determined the course of its history. The recent assassination of King Alexander of Yugoslavia, as an instance, was committed by members of one of these groups from the Balkan area. The killing of Archduke Ferdinand at Sarajevo in 1914 was laid by Austria to a Serbian secret society—and this event led to the outbreak of the World War.

In the Balkans, the Imro—Internal Revolutionary Macedonian Organization—is a leader in the terrorist movement. The Protogeroffists, another group of Macedonians, has also been a powerful political factor in that section. Also in Yugoslavia there is the Ustasha, whose leaders were recently seized.

Rumania's Iron Guard, a fascist organization, was responsible for the slaying of Premier Ion G. Duca. In Northern Europe perhaps the best known

Shots blasted inside the house. Jimmy Christopher broke off in alarm. He sprinted toward the huge dwelling, while Tim Donovan ran at his side. Lights flashed on in the lower rooms while Intelligence men swarmed through open doors. Again shots cracked, and hoarse cries sounded. Jimmy Christopher hurried into a huge, paneled library.

The Intelligence operators had searched the house. Their drawn guns had made captives of the few men they found hiding in the rooms. Two in mechanic's coveralls were being forced against the wall, arms upraised, when Operator 5 entered. Other men appeared, forcing four more prisoners before them. Jimmy Christopher straightened with a grim smile as he studied the lean, evil face of the foremost.

"We meet again, Apito," he said quietly. "You are in the custody of the United States Government."

---

secret revolutionary organization was the Irish Republican Brotherhood, or Sinn Fein.

The forerunner of all present day secret societies was the Carbonari—literally "charcoal burners"—of Southern Italy, formed early in the nineteenth century. Although King Ferdinand IV tried to abolish the Carbonari, it flourished and spread to France. Lord Byron was one of its members, and Louis Napoleon, later Napoleon III, was a sympathizer. It paved the way for Italy's internal wars and revolutions of the nineteenth century.

The most dangerous and far-flung secret societies of today function under such close cover that details concerning them are meager and uncertain, but there can be no doubt of their existence.

Apito snarled. "You think you can force me to talk?" he challenged. "I will say nothing."

Operator 5's lips tightened as he scanned the faces of the six captives.

"Look at them, Chief! They are Latins and Slavs. They cannot possibly bear any allegiance to Great Britain—yet that is the basis on which the Secret Loyalists existed since our independence. These are Jobert's lieutenants."

"Then Jobert has seized the leadership of the Secret Loyalists in order to use their death-ray weapon against the United States!"

Tim Donovan tugged anxiously at Operator 5's sleeve. "Jimmy, listen! Before I was locked in the hangar, I heard Jobert speak of a plan. He said the force will be turned on the Atlantic Fleet tomorrow. They're going to—"

"What!" Z-7 stared aghast. "The Atlantic Scout Squadron is engaged in target practice off the eastern coast of Florida. If that devilish power is turned upon those ships—"

"If Jobert promised it," Operator 5 broke in quietly, "the power will strike." His eyes narrowed as his mind sped. "Order a Naval amphibian to be ready for me, Chief. There is no way we can stave off Jobert's next blow—but when it falls, I'm going to be on the scene."

CHAPTER 6
ANCIENT ALLEGIANCE

J IMMY CHRISTOPHER brought the Intelligence sedan to a stop in front of the great War, Navy and State Departments Building in Washington, D.C. With Tim Donovan, he had taken off from Jay Field, New York, at dawn, in the plane assigned to his special use. The service machine had met him at Bolling Field. It waited ready to return to the flying post, so that he might swiftly resume his flight to the target practice area off the coast of Florida.

Operator 5 strode with the Irish lad into the War Department section of the building, where he rapped on a door lettered: *War Plans Division*, and entered. He found Major-General Falk, Chief of Staff, about to step out. Falk eagerly seized his hand.

"I'm vastly relieved to see you, Operator 5. General Braxton is still missing. We haven't found the slightest clue to his whereabouts. I beseech you to do everything possible to find him."

"I'm here, General," Jimmy Christopher answered, "to discuss the case with his brother. With your permission, I will see Captain Braxton alone."

"But the Captain is completely at a loss," Falk protested. "He can give you no help. I have conducted the investigation personally and I am better able than he—"

"I am not so interested in learning *where* General Braxton is," Jimmy Christopher interrupted cryptically, "as *what* he is."

He strode past while Major-General Falk stared in bewilderment. He knocked at a door and opened it at once. Tim

Donovan followed him alertly into the inner office. A ruddy-faced man rose from a desk as they approached. He studied their faces puzzledly, with growing apprehension, during a moment of silence, until Operator 5 spoke softly:

" 'Long live the King!' "

Captain Braxton's face instantly became deathly white. His lips mumbled upon soundless words. Despair shone in his eyes as he straightened. Operator 5, smiling wryly, said in the same gentle tone:

"I am investigating the disappearance of General Braxton. Or perhaps I should say—the disappearance of the man whose name is the same as yours—Brennock."

The captain blurted in terror: "You know?"

Jimmy Christopher leaned across the desk tensely. "I know the man called General Braxton left New York in an army pursuit plane last night presumably for Washington. I know that, instead, he flew to a hidden field in Eastern Pennsylvania. His purpose was to direct the further destructive activities of the undercover society called the Secret Loyalists. He is responsible for the disruption of the air maneuvers and the death of hundreds. You, captain, have worked at his side in a diabolical plan to render the United States defenseless."

The man known as Captain Braxton stared appalled.

"Do you deny that you and your brother, while acting as members of the Joint Board of the United States Army and Navy, have actually planned to destroy this nation?"

The captain straightened. "I do not deny it."

"It is well that you do not," Jimmy Christopher returned,

"because I know it's a fact. Your brother has put these destructive plans into operation—plans which have been building for a century and a half."

THE CAPTAIN'S lips curled. "Operator 5, you have learned the secret too late. During a hundred and fifty years, our work has never ceased. We have the power to turn back the pages of history and return this land to the dominion of the Crown. Nothing can halt us now."

He leaned forward, eyes shining desperately. "I have no fear of your knowing the whole truth. My brother's name, and mine, as you guessed, is not Braxton. It is Brennock. It is older by far than this nation, and it carries with it a great pride and a great cause. Our heritage is the secret allegiance of Major Lloyd Brennock to the Crown of England. We have never failed it. We cannot fail it now!"

Operator 5 said softly: "You are too sure."

The man at the desk smiled defiantly. "You do not know the strength of blood and faith. Major Brennock's secret loyalty to the King did not cease with treaties. Because he received no royal orders to cease his endeavors, he ignored the Treaty of Yorktown. He continued to fulfill his pledge—to do all in his power to preserve these colonies for His Majesty the King— until death claimed him. On that day, his son took up his task. It has been handed down through generation after generation, until now it rests in the hands of my brother—the man known as Brigadier-General Braxton."

Operator 5 remained grimly silent as the white faced man rushed on:

"We entered the United States army in order to further our purposes. We assumed these posts because they enabled us to complete our plans. We owe only one allegiance—to our name and the King. We know only one purpose—that of the man whose blood flows in our hearts. Our heritage is that of Mother England, and we have kept it pure. I repeat your salutation, Operator 5: 'Long live the King!'"

"And you," Jimmy Christopher asked quietly, "have stood ready to assume the leadership of the Secret Loyalists when death took it from the hands of your brother. You have planned to bequeath it to your son when you in turn passed on. I am afraid—"

"After one hundred and fifty years," the answer came gravely, "our plans have suddenly crystallized. We no longer look forward to our hour of victory—because the hour is here! We have chosen a time when we possess the power—when a world situation urges our use of it. Watch the new history written day by day, Operator 5. The flames of war will encircle the globe, and when they die down, the most powerful of all nations will again hold dominion over these colonies—Great Britain!"

Operator 5's eyes grew darkly solemn. "I do not for a moment condone your secret purpose or your destructive work, captain, but I cannot refrain from paying respect to your loyal devotion. However mad and enduring your cause may be, it is no stronger than my own loyalty to the nation you are attempting to destroy. I can sympathize with you and pity you—because you have lost."

"No! We will achieve our purpose and—"

"Lost!" Operator 5 snapped, leaning forward. "The society of the Secret Loyalists no longer carries on the traditional cause of Major Brennock. It no longer pays allegiance to England. Your brother is no longer its leader. He has forfeited his heritage to one who is as deadly an enemy of Britain as of the United States. Do you know, captain, the name of Arnes Jobert?"

THE MAN at the desk echoed in confusion: "Jobert?"

"He is now the leader of the Secret Loyalists. I saw him take your brother prisoner last night. I saw men in black robes, wearing the symbol of the Diamond Crown, obey his orders. Jobert has destroyed the instrument of your devotion and made it an evil thing. His purpose is the same—to destroy the United States—but not in the name of Britain. Not in the name of any existing power! His plan is to build up a dictatorial, radical government over which he will hold supreme command! That is why, captain, I say your case is lost!"

The captain demanded breathlessly: "Is that the truth?"

"It is true."

The man known as Braxton stared stricken. The incredulity shining in his eyes gave way to unwilling belief. Operator 5 knew that the disappearance of Brigadier-General Braxton was convincing him. He turned slowly, as if no longer aware of his surroundings, and moved toward a door behind the desk. Jimmy Christopher strode quickly and seized his arm. He stared as if at a ghost.

"Do you know where your brother is?"

"No."

The man known as Captain Braxton pushed blindly through the door. When it closed, Jimmy Christopher turned to the telephone on the desk. Lifting the receiver, he asked gravely for connection with Major-General Falk's office. The firm voice of the Chief of Staff answered the call. Operator 5 began quietly: "It will be necessary, General, to place Captain Braxton under arrest. The charge is—"

A sharp click, sounding in the adjoining room, halted Jimmy Christopher's words. Eyes widened with alarm, he spun to the connecting door. Tim Donovan sprang to his side as he thrust it open. They were entering swiftly when a crashing report rocked the room.

Operator 5 stopped stiffly, gazing stunned at the man seated in a chair near the window. Captain Braxton had opened a drawer of a desk. He had brought the barrel of a revolver into his mouth. Smoke wisped from his lips as he spilled forward. He slumped to the floor, a trickle of red crossing his ruddy cheek. The revolver fell from his limp fingers as his wide eyes stared.

Operator 5 drew back tensely. He closed the door of the inner office and went slowly to the desk. General Falk's voice was rasping impatiently when he took up the receiver.

"I have a report, sir," Jimmy Christopher said quietly. "Captain Braxton has just committed suicide."

OFF THE coast of Florida, the great, gray ships of the Scout Squadron of the United States navy rode the swells in line formation. Their huge guns glittered in the brilliant sunshine. Their crews were at their battle stations, efficiently obeying the crackling commands of alert officers. Again and again the sea shook as the tremendous cannon spouted flame and fumes. Target practice was in full swing.

The scream of flying projectiles cut through the air in which planes were circling. Aerial observers were spotting the strike of each shell. Explosives roared around the floating target and blue-green geysers sprang from the surface of the sea at each terrific impact. Again and again the guns came down accurately on their mark.

Past the coast, and far inland, lay the brooding green wilderness of the Everglades. The desolate swamp lay silent, until the faint drone of an airplane pulsed, with loudening note, through the steamy air. Wings glittered high against the zenith as the plane approached. It was a naval amphibian which swung from the north and slowly circled.

Operator 5 peered down from the control pit of the lone plane. Tim Donovan clung to the cowling of the cubby behind him. For long minutes they studied the trackless morass below them.

They had left the War, Navy and State Departments Building and resumed their flight. While streaking southward a report had flashed through the wireless receiver of the craft. The information from the Washington Intelligence headquarters had urged Operator 5 to turn his course toward the mysterious watery desert of Florida:

... 36-89... PLANE ORDERED FROM JAY FIELD IN PURSUIT OF FLEEING CRAFT LAST NIGHT SENDS FINAL REPORT... TRAILED TO FLORIDA... CRAFT DISAPPEARED INTO EVERGLADES... CHASE ABANDONED... MF MEN SEARCHING SWAMPS...

REPORT WILL BE RELAYED WHEN RECEIVED…
WDC-13….

Jimmy Christopher searched the swamps from his high vantage point with the aid of powerful binoculars. Though he persisted for some time the thick jungle growths below yielded no hint of their secret. He straightened at last, glanced anxiously at the dash clock, then sent the amphibian driving toward the eastern coast.

The shore vanished behind him. Operator 5 sighted the great ships of the Scout Squadron lined against the horizon. Their guns flashed and thunder rolled as he climbed. Observation crates were circling high above the target while practice continued. Jimmy Christopher pulled to an elevation higher than theirs, and leaned his wings into a smooth circle.

He raised the microphone as he again glanced with growing concern at his watch: "Calling WDC-13."

A voice answered promptly from the Central Intelligence headquarters in Washington.

"Inform Z-7 we are in position near the Scout Squadron. Are there any reports?"

IN A moment the voice of the chief of the Service answered through the ether: "Operator 5! We have been questioning the prisoners taken last night on the Westchester estate. They are all contemptuously defiant, sure of the success of their plan. All are Jobert's lieutenants, and it is true Jobert has knitted every radical group into the most dangerous super-organization ever to threaten the safety of this nation. These men have admitted that the force will strike again today, at the Scout Squadron, at high noon."

"It is not long until twelve, Chief!"

"I know! I have flashed a warning to all ships engaged in target practice. It will be of no avail. It is impossible to shield the squadron in any way. Even if the ships scatter, they will be unable to protect themselves. Major-General Falk would refuse to order them to run from the danger even if it might help. We cannot admit defeat in that way. We must somehow, find those damnable projectors and destroy them."

"Have you already ordered—?"

"I've sent urgent instructions to every headquarters to search the surrounding country. There must be many of the machines, so placed that they can liberate the death star-beams at any of our defense points. Yet I'm afraid the search will be helpless. Surely the Secret Loyalists have taken every precaution to guard the locations and keep them secret. We are ready to order troops out, to seize the machines, if any are found, but—"

Z-7's voice faded despairingly. Operator 5 answered crisply:

"There is one possibility we must investigate, Chief. You remember, the height of the protective layer of ozone is calculated by taking radio soundings. These soundings must be made just before the projectors go into action. Flash the naval direction-finders again to try to pick up the impulses and chart them. That may reveal the locations of the machines. In the meantime, Tim and I are keeping this position."

"I will send those orders at once, my boy. We are standing by for further information from you."

Jimmy Christopher lowered the microphone and again brought his binoculars into play. While the gray ships rolled on the swells below, guns roaring, he scanned the sky. He saw nothing in the clear blue of the heavens until the dash clock indicated only a few minutes remained until twelve o'clock.

His heart quickened when he spotted a lone plane speeding seaward. Its direction revealed that it was driving from the region of the Everglades. As it approached, at top speed, Operator 5 recognized it as an army pursuit. Stirred with the hope that it was the craft of the new leader of the Secret Loyalists, he quickly pulled the stick and sent his amphibian soaring still higher. He leveled at the ceiling, and watched the plane again.

It was howling toward the air above the rolling battleships. Operator 5 was able to see clearly the face of the pilot in the pit. The goggled eyes of the man at the controls were narrowed at the line of formation on the sea. His cold lips were curved in a hard smile. A chill struck at Jimmy Christopher's heart as he recognized Arnes Jobert.

A slight movement in the second cubby drew Operator 5's keen eyes. Amazed, he saw the figure of a man crowded down beside the seat, face turned away. The plane's passenger was bound hand and foot. A parachute pack was strapped across shoulders, and a length of glittering wire fastened the rip-cord ring to the cowling. He was coatless, but his gray breeches were part of the uniform of an officer of the British Regulars at the time of the American Revolution.

OPERATOR 5'S quick glance at the dash clock revealed that only two minutes remained until high noon.

"Watch that crate, Tim!" he warned. "I want it traced back to its point of takeoff if possible. Be prepared to take these controls if anything happens."

Jimmy Christopher kept his amphibian circling back of the position of the gray ships while he watched. Carefully he avoided the region through which the violet beam must pass if it struck the squadron. Yet, with contemptuous fearlessness, Arnes Jobert was flying directly into the region above the battle fleet. His elevation higher than the observation ships, he suddenly flung his crate into a startling maneuver.

Its nose lifted. It climbed at a steadily increasing angle. Quickly it went over in a swift loop. When it was flying upside down, a gray streak shot out of the rear cubby. The passenger of Jobert's plane spilled down from the pit! Bound hand and foot, the man in gray breeches plunged into empty air while Operator 5 watched appalled.

He understood instantly the meaning of the glittering wire which connected the passenger's parachute cord to the cowling of the inverted pit. It snapped tight as the bound man reached its end. The ring pulled free. Immediately, the pilot 'chute flicked out; then the big, silken bell. The captive jerked in the harness and began to float downward slowly.

Tim Donovan exclaimed: "If he falls in the water he'll never be able to help himself, Jimmy!"

Operator 5 leveled swiftly and thrust the throttle wide open. With the engine howling at its limit, he drove down toward the drifting man. He jerked a parachute from beneath the seat of his pit and pulled on the harness as he watched Jobert's plane.

Jobert had completed the loop. Executing a vertical-winged bank, he thundered in the direction he had come. Behind him, the pinioned man hovered on the wind directly above the ships of the Scout Squadron.

For one frantic moment, Jimmy Christopher debated the choice of following Jobert or plunging toward the shining parachute. Deciding on the latter, he tightened the buckles of his pack, and called back through the roar of the motor:

"Take the controls the instant I let go, Tim! Jobert intends that man to be dead when he strikes the water. He deliberately dropped his prisoner into the path the beam must take if it hits the ships. That's the special death he promised!"

With the parachute harness drawn tight, Jimmy Christopher looked at the dash clock. The short time remaining until noon sent a chill through his heart. Tim Donovan had steadied the controls. Now Operator 5 seized them. He leaned the plane in a sharp bank to send it whirling close to the bound man. He raised from the seat, white hands on the cowling, gestured anxiously for Tim to take the stick. As he neared the floating man he tensed to leap.

Suddenly he sprang from the pit. He hurtled through the air with arms outstretched. Deliberately he flung himself directly upon the billowing bell. The momentum of his body forced it to collapse as he gripped the loose silk. The bound man began to fall swiftly. Jimmy Christopher, clinging to the slippery folds, was pulled down after him at a dizzy speed.

He knew less than a minute remained until the instant of doom. With a frantic effort, he freed one hand and snapped

100

away the rip-cord of his pack. The pilots-'chute flashed out. The unfolding silk caught the air and swelled. With the weight of two men threatening to rip it asunder, it slowed their descent. Still gripping the enwrapping silk, supporting the bound man, Jimmy Christopher reached to the singing shroud lines.

With all his strength he spilled air from the 'chute. With the silk fluttering above him, his downward speed increased again. His expert manipulation of the lines sent him sliding at an angle. He peered down, filled with a wild hope that enough time would remain to carry him far beyond the gray ships rocking below.

Each instant an eternity of dread, Jimmy Christopher kept the 'chute sliding downward. He could hear the amphibian circling beyond as Tim Donovan manipulated its controls. Below, the thunder of the big guns boomed. Wind hissed through the straining shrouds of the chute and slapped the silk. The ships were receding rapidly.

Suddenly—the beam!

It sprang out of nothingness, a brilliant violet shaft. Straight downward it struck, a bolt of silent lightning. Its blinding color flashed past Operator 5 as he drifted. His expert handling of the 'chute had swung him beyond its path, but it passed so near the deadly hue struck him coldly breathless. His eyes strained down during the instant of the beam's existence. It played its deadly power over the entire line formation of the Scout Squadron. Then, as swiftly as it had appeared, it vanished…!

CHAPTER 7
PRISONER'S VOW

OPERATOR 5 released the shroud-lines. His 'chute fattened and took a stronger grip on the air. Drifting, while the bound man dangled below him, he stared in dismay across the sky.

The observation planes kept their position a moment. The purplish shaft had enveloped them. The first hint of its annihilating effect came when Operator 5 saw the glittering wings waver erratically. Slowly, yet with ghastly certainty, the crates nosed down.

One broke into a spin that became swiftly more violent. The other went down wing over wing, like a falling leaf. The first dove into the sea with a terrific impact. Broken wings were already floating on the surface when the second crate struck. It slapped into the waves with rending force and began to sink. Operator 5 glimpsed its pilot and observer sitting motionless in their pits as it slid beneath the waves.

Now the great ships of the Scout Squadron rocked in the swells with their big guns silent.

Only the drone of the amphibian disturbed the awesome hush that settled over the sea. Operator 5 saw it circle past him as he drifted down. Tim Donovan, at the controls, peered at him in wild concern. Jimmy Christopher tightened his grip on the slippery folds of silk to support the bound man as the distance to the blue surface melted. He watched while it blurred up, and carefully loosened the buckles of the harness.

The instant the feet of the pinioned man touched the water, he pulled strongly to empty the 'chute. The man plunged beneath the surface. Operator 5 streaked down as the silken bell went slack. He shrugged the straps off as cold gray-green enveloped him. Desperately he kicked up, pulling on the bound man's lines. When he bobbed through the surface, the man in the harness rolled helplessly in the waves.

Jimmy Christopher sensed that the amphibian was coming near as he drew a knife from his pocket. He touched a button and its keen blade sprung up. He bore it against the ropes fastening the unconscious man's ankles and wrists. He jerked the buckles of the 'chute-straps loose. He was supporting the limp man in the water when he glanced across the swells to see the amphibian slashing down.

Tim Donovan shot the crate toward Operator 5. With the motor cut, he clambered over the cowling and reached. Operator 5 guided his hand to the lax arm, pulled up. While water streamed from his clothing, he legged into the pit. Tim aided him to hoist the other into the rear cubby. When the man in gray breeches lay stunned against the seat, Jimmy Christopher straightened breathlessly to search the empty sky.

"The other plane, Tim! Jobert's! Where did it go?"

The Irish lad answered, flustered. "Gee, Jimmy, I didn't even look at it after you jumped out. I was too worried about you. It was heading in the same direction it came from—but it's gone now."

"Okay, old timer," Operator 5 answered grimly. "It's probably down by now. If it ducked into the Everglades, there's not a chance of sighting it. Let's get back into the air."

The boy turned anxiously to make contact. As the moving prop caught, he glanced into the second cubby and asked quickly: "Who is *he*, Jimmy?"

"The officer known as Brigadier-General Braxton."

AN AMAZED Tim Donovan sent the plane skimming across the swells while Operator 5 checked the adjustment of the wireless equipment. As the plane lifted and climbed, he peered back at the gray ships of the line. Grimly, as the amphibian's elevation increased, he spoke into the microphone:

"Calling WDC-13!"

"On the air!" The voice was Z-7's.

"Chief, the death-star beam struck at exactly noon. It hit the entire Scout Squadron. Unless I'm mistaken, every man aboard those ships is now a stiffened corpse!"

Z-7 answered in despair: "We caught the radio sounding signals, Operator 5—the warning that the beam was about to strike. Since then I have been trying to raise the flagship of the Scout Squadron by wireless. There is no answer!"

"Have the direction-finders reported, Chief?" Jimmy Christopher asked anxiously.

"We have just finished checking their information. The lines converge in the very middle of the Everglades. The projector must be hidden somewhere in the swamps!"

"I thought so! I spotted Jobert's plane leaving that region, chief. It means there's a secret field hidden there. I'm going to try to locate it now. Stand by for—"

"Wait!"

Operator 5 listened intently into the humming silence of the phones. The Scout Squadron was receding in the distance while Tim Donovan kept the amphibian roaring toward the coast. The Everglades lay directly ahead, and at their swift speed the craft would soon reach the mark. When, at last, Jimmy Christopher heard Z-7's voice return over the ether, cold amazement filled him: "Your orders, Operator 5, are *not* to search for the secret field. You are to report back to Washington at once!"

"Chief," Jimmy Christopher protested, "I have a chance now to—"

"A message has just been received at this headquarters," Z-7 interrupted urgently. "It is signed with the name of Arnes Jobert. It warns us that if we make an attempt to locate any of the headquarters of the Secret Loyalists, all our defenses will be wiped out, to the last man!"

"We've got to ignore that warning, Chief, and try to find this field while—"

"Good God, we can't ignore it!" Z-7's voice crackled. "We can't doubt Jobert means exactly what he says. He is completely merciless. He'll carry out his threat without the slightest hesitation if we don't comply. It's a risk we dare not take."

"But, chief—!"

"Follow orders!"

The snapping command was followed by a click. Z-7's voice did not sound again. In dismay, Operator 5 kept the microphone poised at his numb lips. Then, slowly, as despair filled him, he lowered it. He turned to Tim Donovan and called through the thunder of the motor:

"Set your course for Washington!"

THE CENTRAL office of the United States Intelligence, designated WDC-13, was hidden behind secret doors not far from the hub of Washington, D.C. Entrance to it could be gained only by agents who knew the intricate passages and code words. The suite of rooms was windowless, so completely concealed from the workaday world that lifelong residents of the capital could not suspect its existence.

In one of the inner rooms, Z-7 and Operator 5 stood at a desk, reading reports that had just come off the wires while Tim Donovan stood by anxiously. The information painted a picture of tragic destruction and death.

"The most staggering disaster we have ever suffered!" the Washington chief declared grimly. "All of these reports came in during your flight back to this headquarters. You cannot doubt now that Jobert is completely capable of making his threat good."

Jimmy Christopher nodded agreement. "He can, if and when he wishes, render the nation completely defenseless." His eyes darkened dangerously. "But in spite of that Chief—"

"We can't take the chance!" Z-7's knuckles rapped the desk. "Here is a report, from the Coast Guard boats that sped out to the Scout Squadron, saying that every man aboard the ships is dead. There is another, telling us that the beam struck a few minutes later at Kelly Field, Texas. Another, saying the beam hit the Naval Training Station at San Diego. Still another, telling us that the Presidio, San Francisco is peopled with frozen corpses. From coast to coast, those damnable projectors went into operation this noon—and we're crippled!"

OPERATOR 5 stood silent, reading other reports. One, from MF, located at Miami, Florida, had come in response to Z-7's orders to abandon the search of the Everglades. It stated tersely:

…WDC-13…NO LONGER IN COMMUNICATION WITH SEARCHING PARTY…THEIR REPORT PAST DUE… POSSIBILITY MEN WERE DISCOVERED AND KILLED…EVIDENTLY PROOF THAT SECRET HEADQUARTERS IS LOCATED IN SWAMPS… ORDERS TO ABANDON FURTHER SEARCH ACKNOWLEDGED…MF….

And another, signed succinctly with a single name, held Jimmy Christopher's eyes.

"We have learned how that message was directed here, Operator 5," Z-7 explained. "One of our New York operators was captured by some of the Secret Loyalists, then released. While he was held, he was given the wire to forward. It is the most insolent effrontery imaginable, but we must heed the warning."

Operator 5 read:

TO THE PRESIDENT OF THE UNITED STATES, THE CHIEF OF STAFF, THE DIRECTOR OF THE INTELLIGENCE:

YOU ARE NOW AWARE THAT WE POSSESS THE POWER TO CRUSH THE GOVERNMENT OF

THE UNITED STATES. YOUR PUNY EFFORTS TO COMBAT US CAN BE OF NO AVAIL. WE WARN YOU THAT, UNLESS YOU IMMEDIATELY CEASE YOUR EFFORTS TO LOCATE THE SOURCES OF OUR POWER, WE WILL AT ONCE DESTROY YOUR ENTIRE MILITARY AND NAVAL ORGANIZATION. YOU WILL SOON RECEIVE ANOTHER COMMUNICATION FROM ME DEMANDING YOUR ABDICATION IN FAVOR OF THE NEW DICTATOR. PREPARE FOR THE MOVE NOW. RESISTANCE WILL INEVITABLY MEAN NATIONAL CATASTROPHE.

—JOBERT

Jimmy Christopher protested grimly: "We cannot submit!"

Z-7 snapped: "We have no choice but to submit!"

He strode to a communicating door. Operator 5 followed him into an absolutely bare room. A man was standing exhaustedly against one of the unbroken walls. The prisoner of the Intelligence known as Brigadier-General Braxton was still garbed in the gray breeches and high boots of the ancient uniform. He straightened to attention as Z-7 coldly faced him.

"You will be held, to face court-martial. Thanks to Operator 5, there is no question of what the verdict will be."

Jimmy Christopher spoke quietly. "You realize now the Secret Loyalists are no longer carrying out their historic purpose. Their true existence has come to an end. You have lost your position as their leader. A century and a half of earnest endeavor has met complete failure."

Stiffly Brennock answered: "That is true." His eyes searched the face of the Washington chief. "Z-7, I am abjectly at your mercy. I stand ready to suffer any punishment. Is it too much to ask now that I be allowed to fight at your side against the man who has destroyed my heritage?"

Z-7 answered coldly: "I can grant you no request."

BRENNOCK WENT on pleadingly. "I mean that Jobert is my enemy, as he is yours. He plans to bring disaster to your government as he has already brought disaster to me. I beg of you, give me an opportunity to help you stamp that devil out of existence. I promise you wholehearted loyalty to that end. I will gladly pay my life if I may only—"

"Loyalty?—you?" Z-7 retorted. "You have distinguished yourself as the greatest traitor to this government in all its history."

Operator 5 turned as Z-7 spoke. "Chief, in the past you have allowed me unusual privileges," he said quietly. "The circumstances demand that I ask another. Since I am the one who took Brennock prisoner, I would like him remanded to my custody."

Z-7 observed: "You realize you will be entirely responsible for him, Operator 5?"

"I do, Chief." Jimmy Christopher alertly studied Brennock's eyes. "If Z-7 grants my request, will you give me your word of honor that you will not attempt to escape me, and that you will follow whatever orders I may give?"

"My word of honor, Operator 5!"

"I must warn you, working with me will probably cost you your life."

"I shall welcome the opportunity."

Jimmy Christopher quietly asked Z-7: "May I consider Brennock my prisoner, Chief?"

"If you wish, yes."

Z-7 turned as a knock sounded on the door. A communications man stepped back as he went out. "The White House on the wire, sir!" Jimmy Christopher remained with Brennock, and heard the chief's voice rumbling at the telephone. Smiling, he extended his hand. Brennock gripped it tightly.

"You may depend on me to the limit, Operator 5!"

WHEN THEY stepped into the adjoining office, Z-7 was turning from his desk. Jimmy Christopher faced him eagerly.

"Chief, it is necessary for us to take desperate measures at once. To bow to Jobert's threat will be to admit defeat. To allow him to believe we are yielding will only encourage him to more merciless measures. We must not waste a moment trying to—"

Z-7 interrupted raspingly. "Our action in this case is suspended. The Intelligence is keeping hands off. We are facing destruction at the whim of a ruthless man, and no other move is possible."

Operator 5 stared in amazement. "Chief, you can't mean we're to allow Jobert to intimidate us!"

"The President and the Chief of Staff," Z-7 went on, "were handed copies of Jobert's warning immediately when it was received. They have just finished a consultation at the White House. Because I have been directing the case against Jobert, they asked my advice. They agreed with my suggestion to suspend action."

Jimmy Christopher protested: "It amounts to surrender!"

"We have taken the only possible step," Z-7 countered. "I have already sent orders to every headquarters to cease searching for the projector stations. All Intelligence men have been instructed to abandon every phase of the case. Those orders, Operator 5, apply particularly to you!"

"You're asking me to stand idle while—?"

"I'm expecting you to obey me!" Jimmy Christopher leaned across the desk earnestly. "Chief, I understand your position thoroughly. You are fulfilling your pledge to do everything possible to preserve the welfare of the nation. I do not question your orders to the other men working on the case, but—please exempt me. Let me go ahead on my own so that we may have some small chance of—"

"You have your orders!" Z-7's eyes shone like black diamonds. "I will enforce my orders drastically, too! If you do not comply, Operator 5, I will place you under arrest and hold you prisoner. You will face court-martial and expulsion from the service, at the very least. That's final!"

Operator 5 straightened. His lips were pressed tightly as he turned to the door. He opened it and signaled the dismayed Brennock out. Pausing on the sill, he sent one grim, searching glance into the stern face of Z-7. Then, without speaking, he went out....

CHAPTER 8
HOSTAGE

O PERATOR 5 strode briskly along the gloomy side-street in the East Forties of Manhattan. With Tim Donovan and Brennock he had returned by plane from Washington. He had sent Brennock to a special destination with strict instructions to await his arrival. He had directed the Irish lad to wait at the home of his father, John Christopher, while he checked reports at Headquarters MW. While there, he had seen information flash in that investigation of the Secret Loyalists was to be abandoned until further orders. He had just left the lofty offices. A desperate plan was forming in his mind as he walked.

A haunting sensation that he was being watched disturbed him. Without glancing back, he paused before a shop-window. Pretending to look at the display there, he alertly studied the reflections in the plate glass. After a moment, he glimpsed the face of a man quietly passing. Jimmy Christopher recognized him instantly as an Intelligence operator working out of MW.

That recognition warned him that Z-7 was having him shadowed, as a preliminary precaution against his pursuing independent work in defiance of orders. Grimly smiling, Operator 5 remained at the window. The warning sense that eyes were upon him persisted. Considering the possibility that he was being doubly watched, he went on. When he paused again, it was to slip nimbly into a dark doorway.

He crowded into the thick shadows as a man approached

rapidly. He saw an oily face, and sharp, black eyes. As the man passed, he caught no glimpse of Operator 5. He was not, Jimmy Christopher was positive, a member of the Intelligence. He glanced about, bewildered, then hurried on again. Clear sight of the man's swart, Latin features convinced Operator 5 that he was also being shadowed by members of the Secret Loyalists!

Grimly he followed the agent who had been shadowing him, then turned abruptly off the trail. Making sure that now he was not seen, he hurried east. He paused at the door of a brownstone house designated Address Y in the secret lexicon of the Intelligence. He opened the entrance, and as his step sounded, Tim Donovan appeared eagerly at the top of the stairs.

"Hello, Jimmy! Diane's on the phone, asking for you. She seems worried about something. Want to talk to her?"

"I certainly do, Tim!"

Operator 5 hurried into the comfortable living-room of his father's home. Diane's voice greeted him over the wire. He asked anxiously: "What is it, Di?"

"Jimmy, I'm not really frightened," the girl answered quickly, "but I'm sure I'm being followed. Someone was watching me when I came into the office this morning, and I saw him again when I went out for lunch. I have just started home, and now I've seen him a third time!"

Jimmy Christopher laughed bitterly. "We're both under observation, then. Is your shadow an Intelligence man?"

"I'm certain he's not. He looks ugly and cruel and foreign. I want to see you, Jimmy, so I'm going to try to shake him and come home."

"Make it quick, Di."

"On my way!"

OPERATOR 5 turned from the phone, anxiously, but his warm smile erased the lines of worry from his face. He gripped the hand of the mild-mannered man who greeted him affectionately. John Christopher had once been designated Operator Q-6 in the United States Intelligence. A serious wound had forced him from the service. Two lead slugs lay so close to his heart that no surgeon dared operate to remove them, yet they constantly threatened him with death if he should over-exert himself. Pride shone in his eyes as he returned Jimmy Christopher's handclasp.

"What progress on the case, son?"

Operator 5 answered, gravely: "The Chief has ordered me to drop it. His instructions tie my hands. But—I simply can't stand idle while Jobert threatens to destroy all our defenses in a few seconds."

"I know."

"Dad, listen." Jimmy Christopher spoke with quiet earnestness. "Going on with the case means insubordination and dismissal, at least, if I'm found out—but I can't stop. I have a plan—a risky chance—but circumstances may force me to carry it out. If I do, will you help me?"

"I'll do anything you ask, son."

Jimmy Christopher smiled. "Thanks, Dad." He sank back into a chair and stared absorbed into space. "There'll be no other way if—" His voice faded, and he sat in silence a moment while Tim Donovan watched him eagerly. When he became aware of the boy's gaze, he laughed softly. "I know what's on your mind, old timer. Want to see another trick?"

"I sure do, Jimmy," Tim answered. "Especially because doing tricks always helps you think out a problem. How about trying it now?"

"All right, Tim." Operator 5 went to a door at the rear of the room. "I've got some new ones that will baffle you. I'll be all set in a second."

He disappeared into his workshop. It was walled with shelves bearing strange devices of which only Jimmy Christopher knew the nature. Here he conducted researches in chemistry, physics and wireless. Here he had made his famous skeleton keys, and various apparatus he used in his work. He used the woodworking bench, and his amazingly complete array of tools in the preparation of his feats of magic. Tim waited eagerly until he came back, carrying a half-dozen spools of thread.

"I'll use Dad's derby hat, with his permission," Operator 5 began. "You see here, Tim, six ordinary spools, three wound with white thread and three with black. Except for the color, as you can see, they're exactly alike. I simply drop all the spools into the hat and shake them so they're thoroughly mixed."

Jimmy Christopher raised the hat above his shoulder so that he could not possibly see into it.

"Now, I want you to choose which color you want me to produce from the hat," he continued. "Of course, luck alone would give me a fifty-fifty chance of being right the first time if I simply took the first at hand. To show you that this is a feat of psychic divination, I will produce a spool of the right color as many times as you care to choose, without making a single mistake. All set? Which will you have?"

"Black, Jimmy," Tim answered.

Operator 5 reached into the hat while he held it high, promptly removed one of the spools, and held it on his palm. "Black it is," he announced. He dropped it back into the hat, and again Tim made a choice.

Men were struggling with
a girl—Diane Elliot!

"White this time!"

"White—and here you are." Jimmy Christopher smiled as he drew the chosen color from the hat without a moment's hesitation. Tim Donovan looked completely mystified, for each time he named one of the two colors. Operator 5 immediately produced it, with never an error. After every choice, he permitted Tim to examine the spools in order to make sure they were exactly alike in appearance. At last the boy blurted:

"You've got me stumped, Jimmy. How do you do it?"

"Simplest thing in the world, Tim," Operator 5 explained. "Listen." He held one of the black spools in his fingers, then turned it end over end. Tim heard a slight tick. "Put a finger on one label, and your thumb on the other, Tim," he directed, "and turn it over yourself." The boy complied and this time, though he scarcely heard the low ticking noise, he felt a slight impact on his thumb through the paper end-label of the spool.

"The whole secret, Tim, is that the black spools have a BB shot sealed in the core. I prepared them very easily, merely by peeling the label off one end of each spool, dropping a shot in, then pasting the label back. When you shake the black spools, you can feel the shot rattle. That tells you the color instantly, because the white spools haven't been prepared at all. And there you are."

"That's swell, Jimmy!" Tim exclaimed as he shook one of the black spools and felt the rattling of the BB.

OPERATOR 5 put the spools aside and drew a number of pennies from his pocket. "If you'd like to see another, using coins in the hat instead of spools," he said, "here we go. First we'll select a few pennies from among these so that each has a different date. There—we've managed to find five, with no two of the same year. Now. Tim, please select one of them at random."

The boy eagerly took a coin while Jimmy Christopher dropped the others into the hat.

"Note the date on it, Tim. Okay? Now hand it to me. It goes into the hat with the others. We'll shake them up so they're thoroughly mixed." Operator 5 suited the action to the words. "Now the problem is for me to find the chosen coin among the others at the first try, through sense of touch alone. What was the date on it, Tim?"

"1902," the boy answered promptly.

Jimmy Christopher reached into the hat while he again held it above the level of his eyes. Almost at once, he selected one of the pennies and displayed it on his palm. Tim saw, as he expected, that the date on it was 1902. Hoping to discover the secret of the trick to be a duplicate coin, he searched the hat thoroughly, but the idea failed him. He scratched his head in bewilderment.

"Even simpler, Tim," Operator 5 laughed. "It's a trick you can't easily repeat, but you can always be sure of pulling it off the first time. I came out here with a small bit of Vaseline under my fingernail. Before I tossed the selected coin into the hat with the others, I rubbed a bit of the grease on one side. That enabled me to find the coin with the right date, literally by the sense of touch. You can use any kind of cold cream or paste for the purpose. A mystifying effort, Tim, achieved in a very easy manner."

Tim laughed. "Thanks a lot, Jimmy. One of these days I'm going to turn the tables and pull off a trick that will fool *you!*"

"I hope so, Tim. When you have it ready—"

Operator 5 broke off, his eyes startled, as a loud thump echoed through the room. It had come up the stairs, as though something had struck the entrance violently. He was moving toward the landing when he heard a short, stifled cry. He burst into a run down the steps as Tim, rushing after him, exclaimed:

"It might be Di!"

Operator 5 slipped his automatic into his hand as he bounded to the door. He heard the sounds of a struggle on the sidewalk. Heels were scraping against the pavement, and guttural voices were sounding breathlessly, when he gripped the knob. His gun was leveled even as he opened the door. His first glimpse was of a glittering gun....

Flame flashed instantly. A slug hissed through the opening. Tim jumped back with a cry of alarm as Operator 5 answered with a quick shot. In cold dismay, he saw two men struggling near the curb with a girl—Diane Elliot. They were gripping her arms, pulling her toward a sedan which stood at the curb with motor running. Operator 5's gun swung toward them, but another blasting explosion blinded him.

The bullet stung his cheek. He jerked the door wide desperately. "Back, Tim!" As he sprang into the open, the motor of the car surged with power. Operator 5 was about to turn his weapon toward it when a warning glitter reflected from the gun of a man crouching near the door. The third shot cracked just as he leaped aside....

THE CAR was speeding from the curb at the movement when Jimmy Christopher's answering bullet wrung a cry of pain from the gunman. The man flung himself forward wildly, arms grappling. His weight fell suddenly on Jimmy Christopher. Crushed against the stoop, Operator 5 had to fight his way clear. He whirled, sent a bullet spattering close to his assailant's head, then sprang to the curb.

Diane Elliot had been dragged into the car. It was already speeding toward the far corner. Swerving past two taxies, it was effectively screened from Jimmy Christopher's bullets. Desperately, he whirled back as the other man scrambled after him. He struck out a straight-armed, powerful blow. The dark man gasped, dropped to his knees, and rolled. Tim Donovan sprang from the doorway and snatched up the gun which clattered to the sidewalk.

Operator 5 ran at top speed along the sidewalk. The fleeing car had vanished around the corner. When he sprang into the intersection, there was no sign of it in the baffling confusion of traffic in the avenue. The attacks upon him in front of the house had kept him from seeing which way it turned. In defending himself from death before the third man's gun, he had not seen the number of its plates. He paused in tortured uncertainty, then hurried back.

Seeing another car waiting at the curb, and divining that it belonged to the third of the attackers, he turned to it.

He found nothing in the door pockets, but when he lifted the rear cushion an exclamation of surprise crossed his lips. He lifted two neatly folded, black bundles. Instinctively, he knew

121

that these were the masks and robes worn by members of the Secret Loyalists. He took them under his arm as he returned to the entrance. Opening it, he paused.

A knife blade had driven into the wood. The steel had pierced a folded bit of paper. The warning message was printed in heavy black type.

TO OPERATOR 5:—

YOUR SECRETS ARE KNOWN TO US. I AM AWARE THAT YOUR CHIEF HAS ORDERED THE INVES-TIGATION DROPPED AND THAT YOU HAVE PROTESTED HIS ORDERS. AS A PRECAUTION AGAINST INDEPENDENT ACTION ON YOUR PART, WE ARE HOLDING DIANE ELLIOT HOSTAGE. IF YOU TAKE ONE FURTHER MOVE, HER DEAD BODY WILL BE DROPPED FROM A PLANE TO YOUR DOORSTEP.

—JOBERT.

Operator 5's glittering eyes rose. "There is only one possible answer to that challenge! My plan goes into action at once!

CHAPTER 9
COMMAND BY PROXY

AS OPERATOR 5'S taxi rolled up Fifth Avenue, he again experienced the uncanny sensation that he was being followed. He had left Address Y after directing that the prisoner be held. With Tim Donovan and John Christopher awaiting his return, he had launched the first step of his plan. His purpose now was to plot his further action on the case—but his psychic warning that he was being shadowed threatened his strategy.

He leaned forward, gave quick instructions to the driver. The machine swung abruptly into a side street. Operator 5 pressed a banknote into the driver's hand and swung out. Immediately the machine rolled away. Jimmy Christopher hurried into the entrance of a staid apartment house. Peering back, he saw another taxi passing. He smiled grimly as it paused across the street.

Shadowed eyes inside it began a furtive watch on the building Operator 5 had entered.

When he stepped into the elevator, the attendant greeted him: "Good evening, Mr. Walsh!" He alighted at the eleventh floor. There was no duplicate of the key he used to open the door of a small apartment He closed the entrance quickly—a portal of steel covered with mahogany veneer—and stepped into the adjoining bedroom.

On an anchored table near the window was a strange contrivance. It consisted of a powerful electric motor, a ratcheted drum around which a rope ladder was coiled, and a black box something like a camera, containing a crystal lens which was affixed to the end of a flexible gooseneck.

Operator 5 quietly raised the window, lowered forty feet of the ladder over the sill. Locking the mechanism, he gripped the rungs and climbed down himself. He descended into a well of darkness. A narrow passage separated this building from the next. At the end of the ladder, Jimmy Christopher swung, caught the rail of a balcony.

He pulled onto the ironwork, released the ladder, and pulled his torch from his pocket. Its thin beam shot upward to the lens of the black box. The ray activated a photoelectric cell which tripped a relay. In turn, the motor began to grind. Quickly the rope ladder coiled upward and disappeared. In a moment, the window slid shut.

Operator 5 opened the French windows of the balcony and passed quietly through an apartment he had rented under another assumed name. This devious means of approach to the penthouse he occupied was a provision for throwing off any possible pursuers. Many times, it had effectively covered his retreat into a personality which completely obscured his identity as America's undercover ace. When he left the second apartment, he was another man.

Rounding the corridor, he pressed a button inscribed: *Carleton Victor.* The penthouse entrance was opened by a dignified manservant, who greeted Operator 5:

"Good evening, Mr. Victor!"

CROWE, GENTLEMAN'S gentleman extraordinary, considered his master a consummate artist. Famed personages from all over the world deemed it an honor to sit before the lens of Carleton Victor's camera in his lavish studio on Fifth Avenue. His signature on a photo-portrait was considered a passport into high society. Crowe, serving Victor faithfully and well, did not dream that the fashionable man-about-town was in reality Operator 5 of the United States Intelligence.

"Good evening, Crowe," Victor answered as he entered. "Have you been well during my absence? I hope you are not overly worried concerning the threat against our national defenses."

"Defenses, sir?" Crowe asked. His pointed nose twitched in wonderment. "I beg pardon, sir; has something happened? You see, I never read the newspapers and I know nothing—"

"An abominable habit, Crowe," Victor interrupted sternly. "An armed enemy could come to this very door, and you would never know it."

"My world, sir," Crowe answered with dignity, "is inside the walls of this apartment. I have no other interest than serving you to the utmost of my ability. I hope you are not displeased, sir?"

Victor sighed. "I sincerely hope I never lose you, Crowe," he replied. "For never in all my life would I be able to find another man like you."

"Thank you, sir," Crowe said with a pleased twitter.

Victor dismissed him, opened the door of a closet. It was completely soundproof. Once inside it, Carleton Victor again became Operator 5. The special telephone in this space was used only for official purposes. Over it he called the number of Headquarters MW, and asked for Z-7.

He knew that the Washington chief had come to New York concerning another case. Z-7 answered promptly. Operator 5 lowered his tone and spoke with an accent unnatural to him.

"Chief, this is H-8 reporting. I have important information that I must bring to you personally. I'm afraid I'm being watched. Rather than risk revealing the location of MW, will you meet me outside headquarters?"

"If necessary," Z-7 said. "What is the nature of this information, H-8?"

"The man who has been shadowing me," Operator 5 countered in the same, disguised voice, "is in the next telephone booth right now, trying to listen. I don't dare tell you here. I'll shake him by the time I meet you." He whispered a street address. "In twenty minutes, Chief?"

"Very well."

Operator 5's eyes shone shrewdly as he stepped from the soundproof closet. He walked along a hallway to a room which, to Crowe's mystification, he kept constantly locked. He entered quietly, and came out a moment later carrying a small leather-covered case. He was again in the living-room, slipping into his topcoat, when Crowe appeared and hastened to assist him.

"Permit me, sir! Your dinner, sir—I am preparing it now."

Victor sighed again. "Crowe, I realize my dinner is the most important event of the day to your way of thinking. Governments may crash, volcanoes may erupt and bury thousands, earthquakes may destroy whole cities, but nothing is more vital to you than my dinner. I am flattered, Crowe, and sorry I can't stay. I would like nothing better than to linger over one of your exquisite fillets, but—alas!"

Crowe looked grieved. "Very well, sir," he said in a wounded, but resigned, tone.

"And Crowe," Victor paused as he opened the door, "don't count on me for dinner tomorrow. Nor the next evening. Nor the evening after that. In fact, Crowe, it would be prudent of you not to expect me for dinner ever again until I actually return. Good-night."

Crowe's sharp nose lifted in dismay as Victor strode out. In complete bewilderment, he remained staring at the closed door while Victor's footfalls in the corridor echoed away.

WHEN OPERATOR 5 emerged from the entrance, he noted, with an ironic smile, that the agent of the Secret Loyalists was still covertly watching the building next door.

He hurried to Madison Avenue and signaled a taxi. It zigzagged eastward with him while he glanced anxiously again and again at his watch. The report of "H-8" was almost due, and the time of the meeting with Z-7 almost at hand when he left the cab at a dark corner near the East River. He stepped through a gloomy doorway, turned to another in a dimly lighted hall, delivered a code knock on the greasy panels, and stepped through into a small room.

It was one of several small apartments which Operator 5 secretly maintained in Manhattan for use in emergencies. Its interior gave sharp contrast to the squalor of the neighborhood. It was modernistically furnished in excellent taste, soundproof, air-conditioned, amazingly comfortable. Its sealed windows and its steel door gave it the strength of a fort. His knock had been answered by the man once known as Brigadier-General Braxton.

"Z-7 is coming here, Brennock," Jimmy Christopher told him quickly. "We're forced to undertake a dangerous plan. It may lead us to Jobert, or it may mean our death. You'll chance it with me?"

"Willingly!"

"Good! Listen carefully."

Operator 5 rapidly outlined his plan while Brennock listened with widening eyes. He glanced several times at his watch. He paused abruptly as a small lamp on the desk flashed on, then off, without a hand having touched it. It was a signal that someone was approaching the entrance to this luxurious hideaway. Immediately, Jimmy Christopher gestured Brennock to step aside, and spun to the wall at the side of the door.

He turned the knob and opened it "Come in, Chief!" he called quietly. He saw Z-7's puzzled eyes through the door. The chief stepped in slowly. Operator 5 made two quick moves at the same time. He nudged the door shut and turned to face Z-7 with drawn automatic.

"Z-7, you're my prisoner!"

The chief stared in amazement. "What the devil do you mean? This is most irregular! I came here to receive a report from H-8. If you actually hold me here, it will be—"

"An offense for which I may be punished by expulsion from the service, and imprisonment—I'm aware of that chief," Operator 5 finished tightly. "I confess I tricked you into coming here by a false message. I am really going to hold you captive. Furthermore, I'm going to disobey your orders to keep hands off the case. I'm following it up, Chief—now!" Z-7 straightened grimly. "I shall be sorry to lose you, Operator 5. You have been my best agent. But now—"

"I'll take the consequences, Chief." He stepped forward, gun twinkling. "Don't attempt to stop me. I won't hesitate to shoot you if it's necessary. You're going to stay here indefinitely. You'll find that chair behind you most comfortable."

A THRUST of Jimmy Christopher's gun forced Z-7 back into the easy chair. His hand moved swiftly to the chief's armpit holster, and he stepped back with a second automatic. He handed it to the amazed Brennock as he retreated to the door, his own weapon still leveled.

"It's impossible to escape from this room, Chief. The walls are so strong a wrecking crew couldn't break them down in a week. This door is impregnable, even to an acetylene torch. You might shout at the top of your lungs, but you wouldn't be heard. The telephone is useless to you because the secret switch which controls it is outside. In short. Chief, you may consider yourself hopelessly a prisoner."

Z-7 glared malevolently. At Operator 5's signal, Brennock took up the case he had brought to the fortified room.

"But I'm sure you'll find it most pleasant," Jimmy Christopher continued. "There are excellent provisions in the pantry. The books in the shelves are the best. The radio and the phonograph will provide you with entertainment and the finest music. You will find a small motion-picture projector over there which will amuse you with the classics of the screen. I think, Chief, I almost envy you!"

Jimmy Christopher quickly opened the door. His gun held Z-7 back while Brennock slipped out. When he drew the entrance shut, great bolts automatically clicked into place. He smiled tightly as he strode with Brennock into the gloomy street.

"We're ready for the next step!"

Brennock gasped: "You've gambled your whole career!"

"I'm not thinking of that now, Brennock," Jimmy Christopher answered wryly. "My job is to defend my country. I'm going to do it, in spite of the Chief!"

A taxi carried them around corners, into the quiet cross-street in the East Forties where Address Y was located. A quick response came when Operator 5 entered with Brennock. Tim Donovan bounded down the stairs. John Christopher hurried into the room when Operator 5 and Brennock entered.

Operator 5 looked a long moment at his father. "When I first spoke of my plan, you said you'd help me. Are you still willing to do that, regardless of what it means?"

"More than willing!"

"Good! Come with me, Dad. Brennock, stand by. Tim, you can help me." While Brennock remained in the living-room, Operator 5 led his father and the Irish lad to a cubicle in his workshop. He gestured John Christopher into a chair in front of a mirror and clicked on bright lights. Opening the case he had brought, he quickly removed bottles, brushes, pencils. He studied his father's face, then set to work.

As intent as a sculptor modeling a head, he wrought amazing changes in John Christopher's appearance. With the soft brushes, he applied basic tints to his father's skin. With bits of fish-skin, so thin they were scarcely visible, he subtly changed the shape of his father's eyes and the contour of the cheeks. Deftly he applied color over small bits of shaped plastic of special composition. Little by little, the features of ex-Operator Q-6 were erased.

A FEW more deft touches and Jimmy Christopher grayed the hair at John Christopher's temples. He blackened the remainder with special dye, and applied it also to the eyebrows. Expert touches played silvery lights on it. Lastly Operator 5 placed drops, with the utmost care, in John Christopher's eyes. While Tim watched in amazement, the color of the pupils darkened. When Jimmy Christopher stepped back with grim satisfaction, the man sitting before the mirror was a new person.

He opened the door, and John Christopher stepped into the living room. Brennock jerked up from a chair and stood staring in amazement. He blurted: "Z-7!"

"Good!" Operator 5's tight smile grew. "To all appearances, my father is Z-7—and he will continue to be Z-7 as long as he can keep up the deception." He turned eagerly to ex-Operator Q-6. "Dad, you are now the commander-in-chief of the United States Intelligence!"

"I'll do my best to carry it through, son," John Christopher promised gravely.

"Now there's no time to waste," Operator 5 exclaimed. "Brennock, you're to stay here until I phone orders. Tim, you're coming along with us. Let's go, Dad."

They hurried down the stairs and out the entrance. Tim marveled at the perfection of John Christopher's disguise. Operator 5's father had worked under Z-7 for many years prior to his forced retirement from the Intelligence. He knew every mannerism of the chief. Had Tim Donovan not seen the change wrought before his eyes, he would have been completely deceived by the man riding beside him in the cab. Yet, when

Operator 5 directed the driver to the skyscraper in which Head-quarters MW was located, they faced a sterner test.

The public elevator carried them to a high level. Another, used only by the Intelligence, was waiting. The guards passed John Christopher at a glance. When they strode into Z-7's office, in the secret suite, undercover agents greeted Operator 5's father with "Good evening, Chief!" His darkened eyes shining with satisfaction, John Christopher went at once to Z-7's desk.

He found reports waiting. Reading them swiftly, he passed them to Operator 5. The first was:

> … WDC-13… SEARCHING PARTY SENT INTO EVERGLADES STILL MISSING… NOW CERTAIN THAT A SECRET STATION IS HIDDEN IN SWAMPS… WHEN DO WE CONTINUE INVESTIGATION?… MF (Miami)….

Another:

> … WDC-13… EARLIER INVESTIGATIONS INDI-CATE SECRET CAMP IN IMPERIAL VALLEY NEAR SALTON SEA… BELIEVE THIS TO BE LOCATION OF PROJECTOR WHICH TURNED DEATH BEAM ON SAN DIEGO NAVAL BASE… MUST WE STILL KEEP HANDS OFF?… LAC (Los Angeles)….

Operator 5 rapidly read other information which hinted suspicious activities at secret spots in the Canal Zone, at a point close to Boston, still another near Death Valley. The swift work of the Intelligence had promised progress until Z-7's abrupt orders had suspended all investigations. Jimmy Christopher's eyes shone with desperate hope as he spoke across the desk.

"Z-7, please communicate with the President and the Chief of Staff." As John Christopher took up the desk phone and gave directions to the communications-chief, Operator 5 went on, rapidly outlining the steps to be taken. His father listened alertly over the receiver and reported: "Falk is at the White House, in conference with the President."

"Excellent. Talk to him now!"

JOHN CHRISTOPHER'S voice simulated that of Z-7 on the line. "General Falk, our investigations promise results. I realize it is running a terrific risk, but I'm convinced we must go ahead. I am directing Operator 5 to prepare a plan to destroy the death-star-ray liberators. We are proceeding at once."

Falk snapped: "Good God, man! If Jobert learns of this, it will mean annihilation!"

"This is a time for action, General, not argument," John Christopher returned.

"But if it fails—?" Falk rasped.

"We face then no worse disaster than if we had never attempted it! Please advise the President."

Operator 5 waited tensely. John Christopher heard a grave, soft voice come next over the line. It was that of the Chief Executive of the nation.

"Z-7, the success of your plan depends on Operator 5 alone. It may mean salvation, or utter annihilation, but you have my consent!"

"Thank you, Mr. President."

John Christopher lowered the phone slowly. Operator 5 straightened, his smile tight, his eyes gleaming.

"In the rest of my plan, Tim and Brennock will cooperate. We will need a fast plane. Will you please order it at my disposal at once? The rest of our equipment is prepared. The wireless communications-unit is to remain in touch with the plane constantly. We will have only one means of reaching you, and everything will depend on it."

Jimmy Christopher turned then to a chart-case at the side of the room. He drew out a thick folder of photographic maps. Turning to an area that pictured the swamp region of Florida, he studied it intently while he made rapid calculations on a pad. He straightened to say:

"A message to MF. Please direct their best men to proceed, under cover of darkness, to Point 56-32 on Map 754K. They will use a boat and tow a canoe. This must be done in strictest secrecy. Instruct them to look for a light signal from the sky as soon as they are in position. They must be prepared to pick up two men descending by parachute. Those orders should go out at once."

"They will be on the wire in a few seconds. Are there other orders?"

Operator 5 answered softly: "No. That is all. The rest is up to me."

John Christopher extended his hand. His son gripped it tightly as he said: "Good luck, Operator 5!"

Eyes shining, Jimmy Christopher answered: "Thanks— Chief!" He went out the door quietly, with Tim Donovan— facing the most dangerous and most vital mission of his career....

CHAPTER 10
JUNGLE JEOPARDY

HEAVY DARKNESS shrouded the watery wilderness of the Everglades. It lay a brooding, black morass which had withstood every advance of civilization. Though great cities and fashionable resorts were located not far distant, a barbaric secrecy walled it. In the very midst of a modern world, it remained a trackless jungle teeming with danger.

High in the night sky, a lone plane droned into the swamp region. From its lofty vantage-point, the Everglades appeared to be a baffling black blanket. Two men peered down at the trackless, pitch-dark terrain while a boy expertly handled the controls.

Tim Donovan, under Operator 5's orders, had sent the plane driving toward the point designated 56-32 on Map 754K. An entire day had passed since their departure from New York. During the anxious hours of waiting for darkness, Jimmy Christopher had fully checked all his preparations. His most careful planning could not exclude a perilous element of uncertainty, but his determination had not flagged. With the coming of night, they had launched into the air, their destination the savage wilderness.

Jimmy Christopher brought a microphone to his lips while Brennock stood by and Tim Donovan kept the crate deadheading.

"Calling WDC-13!"

John Christopher's voice, flashing through the ether from Washington, was exactly like that of Z-7. "We're with you!"

"We are flying into position," Operator 5 reported. "In a moment we'll use the 'chutes. Have you any new information?"

"Major-General Falk has issued secret orders in compliance with our plan, Operator 5. Troops and planes are ready at the army posts and flying-fields nearest the known locations of the projectors. They will go into action at your signal, but first, they must have specific information. We are depending on you for that!"

Tim Donovan looked up from the dash to exclaim: "In position, Jimmy!"

"In position!" Operator 5 repeated over the air. "WDC-13, stand by!"

He checked the reading of Tim's instruments, then signaled Brennock. His prisoner turned a torch downward. Its concentrating lens was shielded in a long black tube so that its narrow beam could be seen in only one direction. Pointing it straight downward, Brennock tapped the contact. The lens flashed a coded flicker. Alertly, while Tim Donovan kept the plane circling slowly, its motor revving as slowly as possible, Jimmy Christopher peered overside.

"No answer!" Brennock blurted.

"The men from MF must be somewhere below. Keep flashing them. The trees are so thick it may take—there!"

Operator 5's keen eyes had caught a faint twinkle in the baffling blackness. It was a mere spark of light that appeared and vanished—but it came again, answering Brennock's torch. Immediately, Operator 5 ordered the signal changed. A new series of flashes shot from the sky: *Coming down!*

136

Jimmy Christopher had already tightened the straps of a parachute-pack around his shoulders. Brennock was wearing another. Operator 5 brought up a black bundle from the pit. It consisted of the two robes, marked with the symbol of the Diamond Crown, which he had seized from the car of the Secret Loyalist agents the night before. He held it tightly under one arm as he leaned forward to speak to Tim.

"Old timer, you have your instructions. You have enough fuel to keep yourself in the air the rest of the night. You're to watch for further code signals from the ground. Whatever information you pick up from us, relay at once to WDC-13. There may be wireless equipment in the station below, but unless I'm able to reach it, the light will be absolutely our only way of keeping in touch with headquarters. Remember, the whole plan will fail unless our information gets through. Tim."

"I know, Jimmy! I'll do my best!"

OPERATOR 5'S eyes grew solemn. "Keep your position as long as darkness covers you. If by any chance you catch no light signals, make no further attempt to reach us, because it will be futile. Worse, it may provoke an attack by Jobert which will destroy our entire army and navy. You understand that?"

The boy pressed his lips tight to prevent their trembling. "Okay," he added quietly as he gained control of himself. "You can count on me to follow orders."

Jimmy Christopher offered his hand. "So long, old timer. I'll be seeing you!"

The boy warmly returned the grip.

Grimly, Operator 5 straightened. Brennock had pocketed

the torch and was poised near the cowling. Jimmy Christopher raised himself into the wind, and searched the thick darkness spreading below. The faint spark of the ground signal was continuing. While the wings of the plane leaned, he clambered over to the step, holding on with one hand. He flashed a smile at the anxious lad at the controls—and dropped....

He vanished almost instantly in the blackness. Brennock, intently listening, heard the snap of the pilot-'chute, then the *poom* of the silken bell. The sounds told him that Jimmy Christopher was floating in the night below. Brennock pulled himself over, gave Tim Donovan's shoulder a reassuring pat, then kicked himself out into space. Like Operator 5, he swiftly disappeared....

HIGH IN the night, Operator 5 swung in the shroud-lines while the parachute floated downward. He knew Brennock must be somewhere near, but he could not glimpse the other 'chute. A faint fluttering of silk somewhere above told him his prisoner was spilling air from the bell and dropping to his level. Operator 5 at once began directing his parachute by skillful handling of the shrouds.

His feet touched soft ground he could not see. Immediately, he fell full length and pulled mightily on the lines to collapse the bell. Footfalls sounded around him as he heard a slapping rustle nearby. It told him Brennock also was down. He groped toward the sound and Brennock came close. They turned together toward ghostly figures that materialized out of the darkness.

"Operator 5," a whisper came. "Everything is ready!"

Jimmy Christopher smiled as he reached to the torch in the

hand of the Intelligence agent who had spoken. "Thanks, D-6. We could never have come down safely without your help. You're quite sure you haven't been seen?"

"We came in, as quietly as possible, after dark. None of us has dared speak until now. We've used the torch only since sighting your flash. So far, you are safe, but we have no additional information. We do not know the location of the secret station."

OPERATOR 5 gazed into the zenith. The blackness of the heavens completely shielded Tim Donovan's plane. Its exhaust was a low drone, so soft it might easily be the whispering of the wind. Jimmy Christopher directed the signal torch upward and touched its contact. The flashes signaled: *Safely down.*

In the sky a star appeared, vanished, then blinked again. Tim Donovan's answer meant: *All's well.*

Jimmy Christopher looked around. Brackish water lapped a few yards away. The surrounding trees drooped slimy leaves from branches that were gnarled like writhing snakes. Tangled jungle growths shivered with the movements of creatures that could not be seen. A pulsing rustling in the greasy grass meant that poisonous snakes were gliding nearby. A sudden splash in the evil water, ending with a sharp click, signified the crushing of a crocodile's jaws on its prey. The night was alive in the swampy jungle....

During his descent, Operator 5 had held the black bundle under his arm tightly. Now he unrolled it, passed one of the garments to Brennock. They shook the robes over their shoulders. The emblem of the Diamond Crown glittered dully in the gloom like the eyes of reptiles. They drew the black hoods over

139

their faces, the black gloves on their hands. The clothing made them blend into the foggy night.

Operator 5 whispered: "Ready."

The men from MF walked slowly across the oozing ground. At the edge of the oily water, they paused. A special boat, its propeller actuated by hand levers, was drifting nearby. The slender lines of a canoe were dimly visible. Jimmy Christopher signaled Brennock into it. Offering his gloved hand to the leader of the MF men, he said softly:

"You've done your bit splendidly. Return to MF as quietly as possible."

He waited on the shore while the undercover agents climbed into the boat. They worked the greased levers back and forth, and the propeller quietly cut the water. The man at the rudder directed the craft along an outlet. Gloom blotted it away. Soon even its slight rippling sound vanished in the constant night noises of the swamps.

Operator 5 kneeled in the canoe. It drifted into the sluggish water, turning. A slithering splash at the bank warned them of the nearness of a crocodile. White fangs gleamed, then vanished. Jimmy Christopher and Brennock began plying their paddles together. The canoe coursed silently along the bank, then turned. The flashing blades drove it still deeper into the heart of the poisonous jungle.

THE TWO black robed-figures followed baffling trails of water. While they searched in coves and skirted islands, a faintly pulsing drone carried out of the apex of the dark sky—Tim Donovan's circling plane. Each passing moment heightened

Operator 5's impatience. While the canoe prowled endlessly through the swampy maze, the night kept its secret.

Operator 5 tensed and listened. In the medley of fluttering and rippling night-sounds, he discerned a soft, rhythmic noise. Turning, he signaled Brennock. The other removed his hood, clipped a disc receiver over one ear, and clicked the tips of its cords into a small connector which led to flat dry batteries contained in his hip pocket. At the same time, he made contact with a web of thin wires which had been sewn in it. He replaced the hood while Jimmy Christopher continued to listen alertly.

Operator 5's gloved hand slipped into a pocket of his robe. He touched a small spring-contact. Opening and closing it in rapid succession, he tapped dots and dashes. The faint Hertzian impulses were picked up by the antenna concealed in Brennock's robe. At each touch of Jimmy Christopher's fingers, on the hidden key, a click sounded in Brennock's phones. The message passing between them flashed: *Boat approaching!*

The rhythmic ripple had come nearer. Paddles gleamed faintly in the gloom. Jimmy Christopher glimpsed the ghostly outlines of a canoe shooting out of an inlet. It sped across the brackish water with no sound save the dipping of the wet blades. In it, scarcely visible, were two figures—being also robed and hooded in black. Operator 5 caught a faint sparkle of brilliants—the symbol of the Diamond Crown—as the craft began to vanish.

He clicked another message: *Follow!*

At once, he sent his canoe gliding after the other. Brennock's paddle sliced the marsh water evenly with his. They sped through the mist, turning as the other boat turned. It was still invisible in the blackness, but the trickling of the swinging paddles led them. They pressed after it as close as they dared—a silent chase through the night.

Suddenly, a white shaft—dazzling bright—cut through the foggy gloom. It originated from a reflector high in the air which, for an instant, was as blinding as the mid-day sun. The beam angled downward at the canoe gliding ahead of Operator 5. Immediately the light flooded over the two robed figures in the craft, they raised their paddles and held them up, crossed. The silent countersign brought immediate blackness back to the marsh.

Jimmy Christopher held his canoe back while the other glided ahead. The rhythm of its paddles vanished. Footfalls sounded through rustling grass. Operator 5 waited tensely until the noises blended away, then they swept boldly toward it.

The white shaft pierced the night again. The searchlight, mounted on a high platform on the island which Jimmy Christopher was approaching, turned its beam straight upon the approaching craft. Operator 5 and Brennock raised their paddles in the countersign of the cross. As before, the light vanished.

Cautiously Jimmy Christopher sent the shell gliding ahead once more. A black bank loomed out of the mist. Ghostly shapes moved along it as Operator 5 swung his canoe close. He was aware of eyes studying him and Brennock sharply as he steadied the craft and stepped out. They peered into the flowing mist, but it shielded all knowledge of their surroundings from them except that they were on an island. There was no gleam of light anywhere, no suggestion that this might be the secret camp—except the many black figures moving along the bank.

Jimmy Christopher's nimble fingers dot-dashed a message to Brennock—words inaudible to the others standing near.

Utmost caution now. Must penetrate to center.

Sharp anxiety filled him as a robed figure came closer in the mist. A throaty voice issued from the mask of the man who paused facing Operator 5! "Workis. Longlo. The leader waits. Special orders to be executed."

Jimmy Christopher chanced the answer: "We go at once."

Brennock whispered an echo: "At once."

THEY TURNED, at a gesture from the other man, and walked through the wet grass. Tramping feet had marked a path through it. They followed the trail, Operator 5 leading the way, through a gloom reeking with jungle peril. At last, when a clearing appeared, they sensed movements and saw other robed men circling about.

The air was tight, as though something of great importance was about to happen. Operator 5 had sensed it on the bank, but here the strange aura of expectancy was even more pronounced. While hooded eyes followed him and Brennock along the trail, they moved past a narrow arm of water that cut deep into the island. They paused peering at a cage resting half beneath the surface.

It was flat and three yards square, with a screen trap-door on its top. The water inside it rippled over things that moved quickly. Jimmy Christopher glimpsed the gleam of reptile bodies writhing angrily. He stooped closer, drawn by a cold fascination, and identified the prisoners of the cage. Snakes! Their markings showed him that they were the deadly, swamp copperheads.

He moved on, with an alarmed glance at Brennock. Now they discerned the outlines of a low, rambling building huddled on the hump of the hill. It was completely surrounded by dense jungle growths that shielded it completely. Near one wall, a group of robed men were gathered. Their eyes flashed through the slits in their hoods, but they did not speak. Turning, they opened the way for Operator 5 and Brennock.

Jimmy Christopher was conscious of a faint luminescence which played over the fabric of his cap above the eyes. He had noted a similar circle on Brennock's hood, at first scarcely visible, but increasing in brilliance. Though he had noticed no marking there in daylight, he realized that a black, phosphorescent paint had been applied. The circles distinguished their robes from most of the others, though several robed men in the group were marked in the same way. The green-glowing circles were a credential which took them through the ghostly crowd to a door.

There another cloaked man, also marked by the shining circle, spoke huskily: "Workis. Longlo. The leader waits. Take your places."

Tortured by uncertainty, but urged by a cold determination, Operator 5 and Brennock stepped through the door. They found themselves in a huge, square meeting room. Its walls were draped with black fabric, so that the candles burning on a table at one side seemed dim. Benches were placed in rows facing the dais. Two other men, wearing the decoration of the glowing circles, were standing beside it. Chancing an error, Operator 5 and Brennock took their positions facing the benches.

SUDDENLY CURTAINS at the rear of the room drew apart. A striking figure appeared and advanced. The lean man who climbed to the dais was wearing the colorful uniform of a British officer of the time of the American Revolution. His boots glistened and his sword shone. He paused, his eyes shining malevolently through the black mask that covered his face. For a moment he did not speak.

Operator 5 recognized the evil mercilessness of the leader's eyes. The man on the dais, almost within Jimmy Christopher's reach, was Arnes Jobert.

"Comrades!"

Jobert's gaze swept over the hooded heads. His attitude was one of fearless command, of unconquerable determination. The merciless gleam of his eyes sharpened as he spoke:

"Comrades! The government of the United States has chosen to defy me. Information has come to our hands, through the tapped wires of the Intelligence, that my warning has been ignored. They are persisting in their investigations. One of their agents is even now attempting to approach this station—the man known as Operator 5!"

Jimmy Christopher's breath stopped. With an effort he kept his masked eyes off Jobert. He listened, chilled, as the leader of the destroyer band continued:

"His attempt is doomed to failure. With that we are not concerned. Ours is a power he cannot overcome—he, nor all the forces of the United States. They have failed to heed my warning, and now they must face the consequences. Our word will be made good tonight!"

Operator 5 was aware that Brennock was staring at Jobert. His eyes were shining with intense, bitter hatred.

"Our death-beam liberators stand ready. Tonight, at my signal, they will act. One by one, the defenses of the United States will be rendered helpless. This government will be stripped of its armed man-power. Every ship, every army post, every flying-field, every coast-defense station, will be peopled only by the dead. We will reign supreme!"

Jobert's words rang into a vibrant hush:

"Then, comrades, our supreme blow! The projectors in the East will cleave the sky directly above Washington! Every official of the government will be transformed instantly into a corpse—from the President to the lowliest page boy! Within an hour, the United States will no longer exist and we shall erect our regime in its place!"

Operator 5's heart grew cold at the indomitable purpose—the merciless drive—in Jobert's voice.

"Your orders await execution. Your comrades hold themselves ready for the supreme moment. Our plan reaches its triumphant culmination tonight. Within the hour. At midnight!

"Comrades, dismissed!"

CHAPTER 11
DEATH MASQUERADE

THE COMMANDING, uniformed figure turned sharply off the dais. Jobert stepped toward the curtains. He paused, and his brilliant eyes turned on Operator 5 and Brennock. He ordered raspingly:

"Workis. Longlo. At my side."

The black-robed figures in the room were moving along the aisles toward the door. No word was spoken as they filed into the misty darkness outside. Jimmy Christopher and Brennock exchanged alarmed glances. Grimly elated at Jobert's order, yet chilled by a realization of the danger they faced, they moved toward the draperies after the merciless leader.

They were followed by the other two men who were likewise marked by the shining circle. As Jobert's boot clicked along a corridor, Operator 5 became aware of a faint humming in the air which suggested that, somewhere beyond, powerful generators were spinning. With Jobert marching ahead, and the other two robed men following, Operator 5 and Brennock strode to a door midway along the hall.

Jimmy Christopher's fingers, clicking the special key in the pocket of his robe, flashed a warning message to Brennock which the others could not hear: *Watch your chance. Take your position as soon as possible.*

The words carried momentous meaning to Brennock. He had Operator 5's planned moves clearly in mind. His part now was somehow to slip outside and escape the eyes of the hooded men.

He was to listen over the short-range receiver for messages sent by Operator 5. By means of the shielded torch, now concealed inside his cloak, he was to flash the information to Tim Donovan in the auto-gyro. Circling high in the sky, awaiting the signals, the boy was ready to wireless the messages to WDC-13. It was the only means of communication they possessed. It was absolutely vital to Jimmy Christopher's plan, and Brennock's part was essential to the system of relay.

Side by side, Operator 5 and Brennock stepped through a door after Jobert. The room was outfitted as an office. It looked like a field headquarters of some general of long ago, Jobert went directly to the old table that served as a desk, and turned his piercing eyes on the four masked men who came to attention facing him.

"Uscott. Allier. We are certain Operator 5 is attempting to get here tonight. Even now, with the help of the Miami Intelligence headquarters, he has penetrated into the swamps. You are to carry word to our observation stations and sentries at once. Furthermore, you are to lead the search for Operator 5. You must find him!"

Jobert's eyes shone like ice filmed over metal.

"Kill him on sight! Throw him into the swamps! Don't come back until you can report to me that the crocodiles have torn him apart! Start now!"

The two masked men called Uscott and Allier turned smartly, and strode from the office.

"Workis. Longlo. You will remain at my side. You are to make certain my orders tonight are executed promptly and absolutely."

Rosvale crumpled under the heavy blade!

A step sounded at the door. Jobert's voice rasped in answer to a knock. A robed man, wearing the symbols of the Diamond Crown and the shining circle, stepped in. He reported briskly:

"The girl."

"Bring her in."

OPERATOR 5 turned in dismay as two other men appeared in the doorway. Their gloved hands clutched the arms of a girl whose face was white with dread. Sight of her shocked Jimmy Christopher breathless. She glanced at him without a suggestion of recognition in her eyes, then defiantly faced the uniformed man at the desk. She was Diane Elliot!

Jobert said harshly: "I made your friend, Operator 5, a promise. He has not heeded my warning, and now he will see my word made good. You will be returned to his doorstep—dead!"

The girl's firm gaze did not waver.

"Dead—!" Jobert repeated with evil gloating in his voice. "You have already seen the cage of the copperheads. You know that once inside it, you can never escape the certain and terrible death it holds. Your lovely body will be scarred by the fangs of the copperheads and bloated by their venom! That will answer Operator 5's futile defiance!"

Jobert straightened scornfully. To the two men who held the girl he commanded: "Keep her here." He snapped at Operator 5 and Brennock: "Come with me."

Jimmy Christopher, obliged to follow, again worked the key concealed in the pocket of his robe, clicking in a message to Brennock.

Slip out at once. I will try to cover you. There is no other way.

Brennock drew back alertly as Jimmy Christopher passed through the door after Jobert. Glancing back. Operator 5 saw him sidling into the corridor, intent on taking a position outside. While Diane remained in the office with the robed guards, Jobert strode along the corridor followed by Jimmy Christopher. When he swung a door wide, it revealed an amazing sight.

Operator 5 stepped into a huge room glittering with machinery. Its floor lay below the level of the island. Its removable roof had been opened, and fog was wafting across the dark sky above. In the center of the room, a great metal reflector was mounted on the machinery of an intricate, directing device. Operator 5 paused, coldly, fascinated, gazing at the doom projector.

He stepped over heavy conduits, following Jobert past the tremendous instrument, and again touched the key in his pocket: *Liberator here!*

Men in coveralls, their faces masked, were moving about the great bowl. Its angle was almost vertical. The hum of generators, louder inside the room, indicated a driving flow of current through meters affixed to the black panels where other experts were on duty. At desks along one wall, masked men were making intricate calculations, using slide rules. One, clad in a smock, his face also covered, was standing aside. Toward him Jobert strode.

"Rosvale! The device is in readiness?"

"Ready!"

OPERATOR 5 recognized the man who answered in spite of the mask. Bernard Rosvale, one of the greatest living physicists, whose name was celebrated in the annals of research. The man's deep-lined mouth was dry and bitter. Jimmy Christopher recalled that Rosvale was a naturalized British subject who had become involved in difficulties with the United States government some years before. Tried for deliberate evasion of the federal income tax laws—again for misrepresentation of himself on his passport—he had been sentenced to a term in the federal penitentiary at Atlanta, then deported.

His presence at this hidden station disclosed that he had secretly returned. Operator 5 realized at once how closely his sympathies must have coincided with the original Secret Loyalists. His previous allegiance had precisely fitted into the purposes of the descendants of Major Lloyd Brennock. Did he know now that the leader of the new Secret Loyalists recognized no such loyalty to Britain? The question was answered in Operator 5's mind as Rosvale spoke:

"For the first time, sir, I must question your orders. Not only because they are unnecessarily drastic, but because, somehow, I have grown to distrust you."

The scientist spoke with quiet fearlessness. Those around him, who heard, paused in their work and stared in alarm. Rosvale peered intently at Jobert's masked face and went on:

"I sense a change in you. You have allowed a personal ambition to overwhelm your allegiance to the cause. I am not serving you as a man, sir. I am devoted to the purpose of the Secret Loyalists, but not to the gratifying of your mad vanity. Do I make myself quite clear?"

Jobert stood speechless with fury. He snapped a name: "Rogiro!" A masked man in coveralls stepped forward obediently. Jobert rattled questions at him:

"You understand perfectly the functioning of the projectors? You can calculate the angles without error? You know exactly the power required and the time necessary to penetrate the ozone strata?"

"Yes, sir!"

"You are able, in other words, to direct the functioning of the projectors tonight as capably as Rosvale himself?"

"Without doubt, sir."

"That is all, Rogiro." As the masked man withdrew, Jobert turned again to the dismayed scientist "You realize your fine principles have made you a traitor to the cause. You are no longer needed or wanted. You have pronounced a sentence of death upon yourself, Rosvale!"

JOBERT'S HAND flashed to the hilt of his saber. Its blade glinted as he raised it with a long sweep of his arm. Rosvale recoiled in terror at the merciless light shining in Jobert's eyes. Operator 5's muscles tensed to fling him forward. Ready to grasp Jobert's wrist and force it back, he realized in a flash that the move would only turn Jobert's wrath on him. It could not save Rosvale in the end. It would, instead, inevitably reveal Operator 5's identity and destroy his careful plan. He held himself back grimly as the powerful blow fell.

Rosvale crumbled under the blade of the heavy sword. His head split; he plunged forward. The keen edge drove so deep into his skull it severed the mask. The scientist's face became clouded with red. Jobert stepped back, eyes glittering, and snapped at the men who stared: "Remove him! Throw him into the swamp!"

Jimmy Christopher stifled his horror as the masked men

came forward. Without feeling, they dragged Rosvale to an exit at the side of the big room. Jobert returned the saber to its scabbard and turned stiffly to Rogiro.

"Check his calculations! Hold yourself ready to project full power at the zero hour. Not many minutes remain until we strike!"

Jobert strode with Rogiro to the first engineer's table. There he bent over sheets of intricate calculations. Rogiro assured him that they were correct. Jobert nodded with satisfaction.

"This position," Rogiro explained, "is close, but not final. The exact readings will be taken by radio echoes an instant before the power is switched into the tube. We will then strike precisely on our mark."

"At the second of midnight!" Jobert rasped.

Appalled, Operator 5 again touched the key concealed in his pocket. He could only hope Brennock had found a suitable concealed position outside the headquarters building. He had no way of knowing whether his message was being received and relayed to the circling plane in the sky. The uncertainty chilled him as he dot-dashed the words: *Affirm zero hour midnight. Targets of projectors still unknown. Stand by.*

Jobert was speaking ringingly to Rogiro. "Tonight my orders are absolute. Every man must follow them without question. Though you may have no full understanding of them, execute them regardless. Events may happen at the last moment to justify changes. In any case, my every word must be obeyed without the slightest hesitancy. You know the penalty for treason!"

"Certainly, sir."

Jobert strode toward another door. Operator 5 had turned to study the calculations of the chief engineer. He had been able to note only part of the readings when he was forced to follow the leader of the secret destroyers. He passed along the corridor to another door, and entered another brilliantly lighted room. ON THE walls, gleaming black panels were affixed. Vacuum tubes were glowing cherry-red. Operator 5 recognized at once that the powerful radio equipment was functioning now. He stepped with Jobert to a desk at which a masked dispatcher sat. Jobert closely scanned a list which had been repeatedly checked.

"Orders have been flashed to every point?"

"Yes, sir."

"Their approximate readings are taken and they are ready to make the positions of the projectors exact for the zero hour?"

"Yes, sir."

"Their calculations have been checked here, so that there is not the slightest possibility of error?"

"Yes, sir."

"Excellent. I must warn you, as I have just warned Rogiro, that my orders are to be executed to the letter, and without question, tonight. If I demand a change in these plans, it is to be put into swift execution. You understand thoroughly?"

"Yes, sir!"

Operator 5's sharp eyes were darting down the column of the lists. He noted the name of every important point of the United States defense. Beside each another location was noted. One was *Everglades*. Another was *Imperial Valley*. A third was *Maine* and a fourth *Rockies*. Jimmy Christopher realized that these designations were the locations of the doom-ray projectors, that the names of the points of defense set opposite were the marks to be covered by each at the zero hour. He coldly straightened as Jobert turned away from the desk.

"Stand ready!"

Operator 5's flexing fingers worked the concealed key: *Exact locations stations still unknown. Order all points of defense evacuated in case definite information cannot be found.*

Jobert turned at the door. "Workis. I will remain at the projector to make sure we strike without error. Return to my office. Order the girl's guards to throw her into the cage of snakes without further delay. They have been given their instructions." The masked eyes sharpened as Operator 5 hesitated in horror. *"Now,* Workis! Do you want to feel the edge of this sword?"

Jobert was striding away, and Jimmy Christopher was turning coldly toward the commander's office, when quick steps sounded in the corridor. Two masked men came hurrying through a door, holding the arms of a third. He struggled to escape, but they forced him along relentlessly. Jobert turned sternly as the two brought their prisoner to a stop facing him. Operator 5 was struck with dismay when he heard their breathless report.

"We've found a traitor, sir! He was hidden near the bank, flashing a light into the sky! He was evidently signaling to an airplane flying above."

Jobert demanded icily: "Who is that man?"

The answer of the robed guards came quickly. One of them reached to the hood of their captive. They jerked it away. A white face shone in the light, darkened with lines of despair. The prisoner straightened, staring defiantly at Jobert, while Operator 5 stood frozen with consternation.

Brennock!

CHAPTER 12
SWAMP PRISONERS

ARNES JOBERT'S hard lips curved into a malicious smile. He stood without speaking a moment, his eyes glittering with triumph. Brennock withstood his stare unflinchingly.

During that moment of silence, despair struck at Operator 5's heart. The communications relay he had so carefully created was broken. The short-range transmitter concealed in his robe could not generate enough to send his signals directly to Tim's plane. Brennock had been a vital link in the system. Now, even before Jimmy Christopher had been able to learn the location of the projector stations, the line of communications had been broken!

"Brennock!" Jobert snapped the name. "You did not come here alone. You were guided by Operator 5. He is here now, in the station!"

Brennock answered grimly: "I came alone."

"That's a lie!" Jobert straightened, his eyes narrowed shrewdly. "Perhaps, Brennock, we can strike a bargain. You do not wish to die, Brennock—do you?"

"There can be no bargain between us, Jobert."

"A small price to pay, to save yourself from a ghastly death," Jobert countered. "A few words, a mere pointing of the finger to indicate Operator 5, and you will live. Otherwise—"

"I came alone! Operator 5 is not here. If he were, I would not betray him. Is that answer enough for you, Jobert?"

Brennock's reply showed bitter hatred. Jobert's lips grew thinner. He spoke gratingly to the men who held Brennock prisoner: "Put him in a boat. Tie weights to his legs. Drop him into the swamp where it is no deeper than his shoulders. Let the crocodiles have a live feast."

"Yes, sir."

"At once!"

The two hooded men turned Brennock away. Jobert was smiling evilly when it closed. Suddenly, eyes flashing, he snapped at Operator 5:

"Do not delay with my orders! The girl is to be put into the cage of copperheads at once. I am concerned with more important matters."

Jobert turned away. Every muscle in Operator 5's body grew tight. Less than a quarter of an hour, and doom would strike across the country. His mind sped as he took a quick, dogged step after Jobert. Jobert heard it and whirled.

"You'll feel this sword!"

The blade flashed up. Operator 5 reached for Jobert's wrist as he glanced around. The corridor was empty. His fingers struck sharply at a point above Jobert's stock. The impact brought instant paralysis. Jimmy Christopher lowered him quickly to the floor.

Operator 5's heart pounded as he straightened. No one had seen his attack on the masked leader. Realizing that robed men might enter the corridor at any moment, he listened alertly at the first door. He heard no sound. Opening a crack, he found the room stored with supplies. He lifted Jobert, stepped in, closed the door and listened intently again.

ANOTHER GLANCE at his watch filled him with desperate urgency. Mind speeding, he stepped out. When he strode into Jobert's office, the two robed men were still holding Diane Elliot. With an anguished glance into her clear eyes, he snapped open another door. A robed man, marked with the shining circle, stepped close.

"Stop them! Bring back the captive! It is the leader's orders!"

Jobert's lieutenant sprang away. Operator 5 turned back breathlessly. Turning to confront Diane Elliot, he ordered her guards: "She is to remain here a moment longer. The leader has changed his plans." When they nodded, he hurried back along the corridor. Every nerve tense, he stepped into the room where Jobert lay unconscious.

He closed the door and clicked the bolt into its socket. Turning, he ripped the mask off Jobert's face. He made sure the effects of the jiu-jitsu tactic would keep Jobert unconscious a short while. With quick care, he removed the man's red tunic. He pulled off the boots, then the remainder of the uniform. After a moment of strained listening at the door, he jerked his black hood away and shrugged off the emblazoned robe.

Acutely conscious of the passing seconds, he got into the British uniform. He poised at the door, adjusting the black mask over his eyes.

He imitated Jobert's stiff stride and imperious bearing as he went to the commander's office. Rounding to the desk, he snapped in Jobert's voice: "Leave the girl here alone. You are no longer needed." The hooded men glanced at each other curiously, but moved together toward the door. They were approaching it when it opened and another, marked by the glowing circle, appeared.

"The prisoner is being returned, sir."

"Let there be no delay!"

A surge of intense relief passed through Operator 5's heart as Brennock appeared in the doorway. The robe had been taken off him. His chin was lifted, his eyes were defiant. He confronted Operator 5 at the desk, lips curling. Jimmy Christopher gestured to the robed men who had brought him.

"Go back. I will deal with this man alone."

He stood motionless until the four withdrew. Once the door closed, he stepped to it and listened. When he turned back, Brennock was poised hands lifting. With a quick movement, he lifted the mask from his face. Another moment of tense silence passed while Brennock stared dumbfounded and the girl gazed wide-eyed as if at a ghost. Then: "Jimmy!"

"Don't speak!" Operator 5 stepped close to them. Diane Elliot's hands clung to his while she studied his face wonderingly. "You're safe as long as I'm not suspected. Stay here!"

Brennock and the girl still stared at him incredulously as he crossed to the hallway door. He went through it quickly, his alert mind formulating a new plan. The impossibility of flashing Tim Donovan's plane forced him to a different subterfuge. He paused at the door behind which Jobert lay unconscious, then strode to the entrance of the wireless room.

TWO MEN, listening through headphones, were attending an instrument which made time-readings of intervals as small as one ten-thousandth of a second. This was the device with which the fluctuating height of the ozone layer in the stratosphere was taken. The soundings were being made when Jimmy Christopher looked into the room. Realizing that the last preparation for releasing the death-star force was being made, he turned away quickly.

He thrust through the entrance of the projector station. A glance at his watch told Operator 5 that only a few scant minutes remained until midnight.

He strode directly to Rogiro. "Change the elevation. Disregard the soundings completely and set new readings. Strike the pitch at 180-180."

Rogiro stared, repeating the figures in appalled wonderment. "That is an exactly vertical direction! The projector will pierce the strata directly above us! It will turn the death force upon everyone on the island! To swing the projector to that angle will mean suicide!"

Operator 5's hand swung to the hilt of his sword. "Those are my orders! Perhaps you question them? You do not wish to follow them?"

Rogiro's face went deathly white. Terror shone in his eyes. He hesitated in frantic bewilderment, but the force of Operator 5's stare caused him to take a recoiling step. He turned slowly to his crew as Jimmy Christopher repeated:

"180-180!"

Rogiro echoed: "180-180."

The crew looked fearfully at the erect, commanding figure in the colorful uniform. His very presence compelled them to obey. The masked men at the helms quickly spun the shafts. Those at the levers pushed, and the great reflector slowly swung. The appalling orders were being carried out when Jimmy Christopher turned stiffly and went out the entrance with heels beating.

"180-180!" Rogiro repeated in a horrified whisper as the door closed.

Operator 5 strode swiftly back to the wireless communications-room. At the desk of the dispatcher he paused, eyes glittering.

"Flash new settings to every station instantly. All projectors are to be scaled at 180-180. These orders are to be carried out instantly and without question!"

The dispatcher stared aghast. The sting of Operator 5's eyes turned him to the men at the panels. He repeated the instructions in a hushed tone. The attendants went pale. Jimmy Christopher's hand moved eloquently to his sword hilt. The gesture was enough to evoke obedience.

He listened to the clicking of the key, intently reading every dot and dash, as he extended his hand to the dispatcher. "The complete list of our projectors, at once!" He suppressed a grim smile as the man at the desk responded by taking a folded document from a drawer. Operator 5 glanced at it sharply. When he turned from the desk, he possessed a record of the location of every doom station.

"Continue transmitting the orders to every site!" he ordered. " 'Zero hour remains midnight.' I can read your signals!"

HIS KEEN ears checked the clicking of the key. The message was repeated while he listened intently. He heard a symbol transmitted which was telegraphic shorthand for "Special attention all stations!" The message continued crisply: "Setting 180-180!" It was being completed when Operator 5 again extended his hand to the dispatcher.

"Your automatic!"

The bewildered man bared the weapon and proffered it. Operator 5 stepped back, releasing the catch, aiming carefully. The two experts wheeled away from their boards as the gun leveled toward them. They backed to the wall, staring in dismay. The gun in Jimmy Christopher's hand cracked sharply four times.

The crashing impact of the bullets wrecked the apparatus. Jimmy Christopher coolly tossed the smoking automatic to the desk.

"You see," he snarled in Jobert's grating tone, "no countermand will be sent!"

His heels pounded as he left the room. He turned again to the entrance of the projector station and paused at the door. Beyond the panels he heard fearful whispers.

"He will destroy us all!" came in Rogiro's tones.

"Mad—stark mad!"

"When the switch is thrown we will all perish!"

"Obeying him means death—we cannot!"

"Rather risk mutiny then—"

Operator 5 thrust the door open. The whispers died while he stared in. The glitter of his eyes cowed the men at the controlling machinery. His lips curled tightly as he spoke again in the voice of Jobert.

"The reading of 180-180 is exactly right. It will remain there. Any man who dares shift the position of the projector by so much as a fraction of a degree will die instantly."

While the men stared, he circled the great platform, making sure of the precision of the adjustments. The bowl was set so that the ionizing beam would shoot upward to a spot directly above the swamps. He stepped back, and again his command rang:

"Detach the helms!"

The whip of his words lashed the crew into action. They rushed for wrenches. Quickly they loosened the set-screws and pulled the spoked wheels from the shafts. When everyone had been removed, his voice crackled another order:

"Throw them into the water!"

He strode to the door and opened the way. The appalled men lugged the heavy wheels across the room and out the entrance. Jimmy Christopher followed them through the fog. They paused uncertainly at a soft bank where slimy water lapped. He repeated his command with a snap. The water splashed as the helms vanished into the ooze. "Back!" he commanded.

HIS HEART leaped as the men hurried through the lighted doorway. He knew that now they would be unable to shift the angle of the projector. It must remain in position to shoot its beam into the ozone strata directly above the island regardless of the elevation of the ionized layer. He strode into the huge station room and placed his hand significantly on the hilt of his sword as he faced the two men who stood pale at the great knife-switch.

"At exactly the second of midnight, make contact!"

Operator 5 strode out of the station the way he had come. With the door shut behind him, he paused to listen again. The whispers were resumed, more breathless, more terrorized than before. "We will not close the switch."

"Then he will do it himself!"

"We dare not touch him if he tries!"

"We must abandon the station—the island—if we can."

"It is too late for that!"

"Too late!"

Grimly Operator 5 hurried along the corridor to the commander's office. Diane Elliot and Brennock turned quickly as he entered. He swiftly looked through the drawers of Jobert's desk as he talked.

"You must follow me. We've got to leave the island at once. The death ray is turned directly on this spot, and I have commanded the switch to be thrown at exactly midnight. If the men obey, it means death for everyone here."

He took a flashlight from a drawer. When he hurried to the door, seizing Diane's arm, Brennock stopped him.

"Jobert? Where is Jobert?"

"In a room down the hall. He may be returning to consciousness now. There's no time to talk, Brennock!"

"A safe escape," Brennock answered tightly, "can mean only a court-martial and a firing-squad for me. My cause is here. Get to a boat as fast as you can. There's no other way."

Brennock turned before Operator 5 could answer. Desperately urged by time, now thinking first of the girl at his side,

Jimmy Christopher hurried on. With his hand firmly on Diane's arm, he stepped into the foggy darkness.

"Quick, Di!"

LISTENING, JIMMY CHRISTOPHER heard a gusting drone from the sky. His heart leaped at the thought that the loyal Tim Donovan was still carrying out orders though Brennock's signals had ceased. Looking up past slimy foliage, Operator 5 could see nothing of the hovering plane. They sought the open in desperate haste.

Near the bank, a patch of open sky became visible. Operator 5 paused, pointing the lens of the flashlight upward. He touched the contact switch, dot-dashing a code signal. *Come down!* He was repeating it when quick steps sounded in the marsh grass, and a black figure marked with the shining circle appeared.

In Jobert's rasping voice, Operator 5 commanded: "Clear the way!"

The black figure did not move from the path. Accusing eyes shone from the slits in the hood. In dismay, Jimmy Christopher caught a glitter of gun metal in a raising, gloved hand.

"We have heard of your orders to set the projector at 180-180. It means death for us all. Now you have signaled to the plane. You are not—"

"Stand aside!"

"You are not our leader!"

Jimmy Christopher bounded forward. Once overpowered and stripped of his mask, escape from the island would be impossible. He grasped the wrist of the hand that held the gun.

He gave a swift, sharp twist that paralyzed the finger on the trigger. A moan of pain burst from the hood of the masked man. Operator 5 jerked the weapon away. His thrust sent his assailant spilling aside. He was stopping, intent on rendering the robed man helpless with another jiu-jitsu blow, when hurrying black figures on the path straightened him in alarm.

"Hurry, Di!"

He forced the girl around a bend in the trail. The water glistened evilly a short distance away as they ran. Boats were creeping near the bank. Operator 5, glancing up, heard the loudening drone of the motor in the sky. It told him Tim Donovan had caught the light signal and was descending. He strode with Diane to the edge of the water and snapped another order to the robed men waiting there.

"Make haste!"

The men on the bank had heard nothing of the spreading whisper of mutiny, but others hurrying now along the trail were bringing word. As they held one of the canoes close, Operator 5 helped Diane into it. He sprang in and pushed off. The girl, grasping a paddle, timed her strokes with his, peering back. Now robed men were gathering on the bank and sibilant voices were audible.

"He is not the leader!"

"Go after him!"

A RIPPLE of water told Jimmy Christopher that the robed men were springing into the other canoes. A dipping of paddles sounded swiftly. He quickly touched the switch of the torch and flashed it upward, toward the growing roar of the descending plane. He heard it swing into a sharp bank—but the gleam made a target for the craft following.

Guns spat. Slugs slashed through the air. They whistled past Operator 5 and the girl and cut into the water beyond. The rattling reports aroused a turmoil along the banks where crocodiles slithered. A caterwauling of night cries mixed with the muffled echoes. Again the guns cracked as Jimmy Christopher sent the canoe shooting into open water.

Tim Donovan's plane was whirling directly above. Again Jimmy Christopher risked flashing his light. The gleam drew the amphibian howling closer. Its thunder blanketed the cracking of guns. Slugs rained again. A bullet cracked into the shell near Operator 5. Another split through at a lower point. Water poured in as Operator 5 labored in the direction of the plane.

The plane settled, slashing toward the canoe, as the propeller revved down. Out of the pulsing of the exhaust, Tim Donovan's voice called anxiously: "Jimmy!"

Straining strokes of the paddle sent the shell curving toward the plane as it drifted. Water was pooling around Operator 5's knees. The level rose swiftly. The canoe was threatening to flounder when a sharp crackle of wood wrung a cry from Diane Elliot. Jimmy Christopher saw her paddle drop from its shaft, broken off by a bullet. Desperately he stroked again to swing alongside the plane.

"Climb up, Di!"

The girl lifted herself, with inky water streaming from her dress. Tim Donovan reached frantically from the plane and seized her hand. The canoe was vanishing beneath Operator

5 when he shifted quickly to a pontoon. Crouching, he aided the girl.

Tim Donovan twisted desperately to the controls as Diane Elliot sank into the rear cubby. Jimmy Christopher commanded "Up, Tim!" as he gripped the cowling. The propeller slashed the air and the pontoons cut white wakes on the black surface of the swamp. Operator 5 pulled himself into the pit with the girl as the amphibian gained speed.

The flame of guns slashed the air. Bullets sang viciously close over the pits as Tim unleashed the full power of the rotary.

Immediately Operator 5 pressed phones to his ears and called into the microphone of the wireless transmitter:

"WDC-13! WDC-13!"

THE THUNDER of the rising plane shook the fog hovering around the secret station. It dinned in the ears of the terrorized robed men crowding around the paths. It reached the ears of Brennock as he circled the gigantic bowl in the projector room.

Every desk and position was deserted. The terrorized crew and engineers had fled. Not a man remained near the huge knife-switch on the panels. Brennock hurried toward the hall-way entrance. He was yards from it when it suddenly opened.

Jobert appeared in the doorway, face livid with rage, eyes narrowed mercilessly. He paused, gripping an automatic in one corded hand. At sight of him, Brennock paused. They remained motionless during one breathless instant. Brennock moved first—a whirl toward the projector.

Jobert's gun spat. Three times, swiftly, flame leaped from its muzzle. Three bullets flew with savage accuracy to their mark. At

The plane slashed toward the half-submerged canoe!

each impact, Brennock staggered. He flung himself in a stumbling run toward the glittering knife-switch.

At the instant his hand touched it, another shot blasted from Jobert's gun. The bullet struck with deadly certainty. Brennock straightened, lips parted in a gasp, eyes glazing with agony. His fingers curled tightly about the handle of the switch. He braced himself, twisting to peer back. Jobert was rushing toward him, intent on flinging him away from the panel. Brennock's lips curved into a smile of bitter triumph.

Indicators leaped in the meters on the panel. A deafening buzzing sound came from the projector. A faint glow filled the fog directly above the bowl. Brennock clung desperately to the switch and peered through the crackling air. Jobert reached his head with the butt of the automatic. Again and again blows drove to Brennock's skull, but he did not let go the switch handle. He gripped it, dying.

Suddenly it struck!

An aura of violet filled the air of the projector station. It descended out of nothingness and endured for one swift instant. With the coming of the color, all sounds of movement around the station ceased. The croaking of swamp birds vanished. The splashing of hungry crocodiles ceased. No step sounded anywhere in the headquarters building. At the panel, Brennock remained a clinging corpse. And Jobert, when the purplish shine vanished from the air, remained with gun poised to deliver a blow he could never strike.

The piercing violet shaft had appeared near the plane soaring above the swamps. Its clean-cut color had split the night, a long beam extending from zenith to earth, for only an instant. Jimmy Christopher had seen it plunge down upon the jungle island and the very projector which had released it. With the thickness of the swamp night again closed around him, he spoke ringingly over the microphone:

"WDC-13! Reporting locations of the death projectors! Signal Chief of Staff to order all men into action! Positions as follows:—!"

The information flashing from the speeding plane was echoed in WDC-13 in Washington and relayed by wire and radio to scattered points in the field....

NEAR THE Salton Sea, California, waiting troops went into action. Trucks loaded with armed infantrymen sped along the desert roads. Pilots threw camouflaged tarpaulins from their crates and soared into the parched night.

In the Rockies, waiting men sprang from sheltered positions. Up steep grades and around perilous curves, a parade of troops advanced. They mounted snowy pinnacles toward an objective fortified by its very position. In the mountains, a storm of attack broke upon another secret station of the destructionists.

Under cover of darkness men and officers had penetrated into the fastnesses of the Maine woods. Only two roads, separated by a hundred miles, ran through these forests, and human settlements had clung close to them. Yet, in the black remoteness, radio signals ordered a drive upon a clearing where another of the infernal death-star ray liberators was hidden.

At scattered points within the United States, and in the Canal Zone, the army and the air corps executed efficient maneuvers.

They swarmed into fortified positions and held their lines. When ordered back by their officers, soaring battle birds dropped vaned projectiles from the night sky. The blasting explosions marked the obliteration of machines built to wield destruction.

By air and wire, reports flashed back from the points of attack.

... WDC-13... IMPERIAL VALLEY PROJECTOR STATION SEIZED... ALL MEN FOUND DEAD....

And:

... CANAL ZONE BASE TAKEN... ORDERS TO ACTIVATE PROJECTOR IN 180-180 POSITION NOT FOLLOWED... ONE HUNDRED FIFTY TAKEN PRISONER....

And:

... MAINE STATION UNDER COMPLETE CONTROL....

And:

... NO LIVING THING FOUND ON EVERGLADES ISLAND... CENTRAL PROJECTOR HEADQUARTERS HELD BY TROOPS....

The relayed messages hummed into Headquarters MW in New York City. As rapidly as they were received, they were flashed to Z-7's desk. John Christopher, his disguise as the chief having been maintained without suspicion, read them with a growing smile. He proffered them across the desk and said with a chuckle:

"Added together, son, they mean that Jobert's organization is wiped completely out of existence. Every projector is destroyed. Regardless of whatever insubordination you have committed, the credit is entirely yours. This—" He added another message as he spoke—"is a request of the President to appear at the White House to receive his congratulations."

OPERATOR 5 smiled tightly. Under his direction, Tim Donovan had flown the plane at top speed toward New York. Fast cars had brought him with Tim and Diane Elliot to Headquarters MW. Reports from the field had already begun to arrive. Now, with the last in his hands, he looked up with grave eyes.

"The long gamble won. I'm content now to suffer any penalty Z-7 may impose upon me. Whatever his decision, he will be justified. This is, I'm afraid, my—my last case!"

He turned quietly to the door. John Christopher, Tim Donovan and Diane Elliot went with him quietly.

They passed corners on which newsboys were howling the headlines of the special editions pouring off the presses.

U.S. Defenses Safe!

All Destroyers Captured!

President Proclaims Salvation of Nation!

Operator 5 reflected as he drove: "We would have lost hundreds of men in the Everglades if Brennock hadn't thrown the projector into action. He lived up to his heritage by destroy-

175

ing Jobert. It was a fitting way for him to die—his hand on the switch that destroyed them both."

He pulled the car to the curb near a bleak doorway. John Christopher was at his side when he entered. He turned to the impregnable steel door behind which he had imprisoned the real Z-7. His eyes were dark and solemn when he inserted the key. He stepped through first, and his father came to his side.

Z-7 rose slowly from a chair. He confronted Jimmy Christopher and the man who was an exact recreation of himself. Astonishment shone in his eyes at the perfection of John Christopher's disguise—and understanding.

He said quietly: "I understand, Operator 5, why you disobeyed orders, and what you have done. You put ex-Q-6 in my place so that you might go ahead unhampered. I have just heard the latest news reports over this radio. You realize, in spite of the fact that your plan succeeded, you are guilty—both of you—"

"I am ready to take my punishment, Chief," Operator 5 said as Z-7 paused.

Z-7's shoulders drooped. "I cannot forget that if I had persisted in my orders, we would now be completely at Jobert's mercy. I was taking the prudent course while you, Operator 5, chose to play the million-to-one gamble. If the nation had crashed, its doom would have been branded on my soul. But in spite of this, you are guilty—"

His black eyes smoldered. As he continued to speak quickly, a broad grin came to Tim Donovan's face and Diane Elliot's eyes shone with a happy glow.

"John Christopher, you are to remain here long enough to

remove your disguise. I am returning to MW at once. While you were there, taking my place, no one suspected the masquerade. When they see me, instead of you, they will not be aware of the change. The farthest thing from my mind is to take credit that is not due me—because it was your courageous work, not mine, that won out—but for Operator 5's sake—"

He extended his hand. Jimmy gripped it warmly. The Chief smiled slowly as he said: "No one will ever know!"

POPULAR HERO PULPS **AVAILABLE NOW:**

THE SPIDER
- [ ] #1: The Spider Strikes — $13.95
- [ ] #2: The Wheel of Death — $13.95
- [ ] #3: Wings of the Black Death — $13.95
- [ ] #4: City of Flaming Shadows — $13.95
- [ ] #5: Empire of Doom! — $13.95
- [ ] #6: Citadel of Hell — $13.95
- [ ] #7: The Serpent of Destruction — $13.95
- [ ] #8: The Mad Horde — $13.95
- [ ] #9: Satan's Death Blast — $13.95
- [ ] #10: The Corpse Cargo — $13.95
- [ ] #11: Prince of the Red Looters — $13.95
- [ ] #12: Reign of the Silver Terror — $13.95
- [ ] #13: Builders of the Dark Empire — $13.95
- [ ] #14: Death's Crimson Juggernaut — $13.95
- [ ] #15: The Red Death Rain — $13.95
- [ ] #16: The City Destroyer — $13.95
- [ ] #17: The Pain Emperor — $13.95
- [ ] #18: The Flame Master — $13.95
- [ ] #19: Slaves of the Crime Master — $13.95
- [ ] #20: Reign of the Death Fiddler — $13.95
- [ ] #21: Hordes of the Red Butcher — $13.95
- [ ] #22: Dragon Lord of the Underworld — $13.95
- [ ] #23: Master of the Death-Madness — $13.95
- [ ] #24: King of the Red Killers — $13.95
- [ ] #25: Overlord of the Damned — $13.95
- [ ] #26: Death Reign of the Vampire King — $13.95
- [ ] #27: Emperor of the Yellow Death — $13.95
- [ ] #28: The Mayor of Hell — $13.95
- [ ] #29: Slaves of the Murder Syndicate — $13.95
- [ ] #30: Green Globes of Death — $13.95
- [ ] #31: The Cholera King — $13.95
- [ ] #32: Slaves of the Dragon — $13.95
- [ ] #33: Legions of Madness — $12.95
- [ ] #34: Laboratory of the Damned — $12.95
- [ ] #35: Satan's Sightless Legion — $12.95
- [ ] #36: The Coming of the Terror — $12.95
- [ ] **NEW:** #37: The Devil's Death-Dwarfs — $12.95

THE WESTERN RAIDER
- [ ] #1: Guns of the Damned — $13.95

G-8 AND HIS BATTLE ACES
- [ ] #1: The Bat Staffel — $13.95

CAPTAIN SATAN
- [ ] #1: The Mask of the Damned — $13.95
- [ ] #2: Parole for the Dead — $13.95
- [ ] #3: The Dead Man Express — $13.95
- [ ] #4: A Ghost Rides the Dawn — $13.95
- [ ] #5: The Ambassador From Hell — $13.95

DR. YEN SIN
- [ ] #1: Mystery of the Dragon's Shadow — $12.95
- [ ] #2: Mystery of the Golden Skull — $12.95
- [ ] #3: Mystery of the Singing Mummies — $12.95

CAPTAIN ZERO
- [ ] #1: City of Deadly Sleep — $13.95
- [ ] #2: The Mark of Zero! — $13.95
- [ ] #3: The Golden Murder Syndicate — $13.95